Those
in
Peril

Those
in
Peril

Stephen G. Hunt

Little Rouge, LLC

For further information, please contact the author at:
srphunt@cox.net

Book design by:
Arbor Books, Inc.
19 Spear Road, Suite 301
Ramsey, NJ 07446
www.arborbooks.com

Printed in The United States

Those in Peril Stephen G. Hunt
1. Title 2. Author 3. US History

Library of Congress Control Number: 2006908095

ISBN 10: 0-9789516-0-3
ISBN 13: 978-0-9789516-0-3

Dedication

To my wife, Rita,
who sustained me during this writing.

To my sons Chris, Brice, and Andy
who encouraged me to complete this work.

To my grandchildren, Delaney and Cameron,
so that they may know a little about their Grandfather.

Table of Contents

Chapter One

Arrival

It was a little after midnight when the MATS bus pulled up to the guard station. The sign attached to the front of the guardhouse read: "Welcome to US Naval Base—Subic Bay, RPI." It was illuminated by one of those yellow high-pressure sodium lamps, so that the yellow lettering looked white and the blue background appeared to be green.

The Marine corporal on duty waved the bus to a stop and signaled the driver to open the door. In compliance, the bus's interior lights came on, temporarily blinding all the occupants that were awake and waking all those that slept. The bus's occupants were all enlisted US sailors and Marines. Privileged personnel assigned to Subic were flown into NAS Cubi Point, an easy motor whaleboat ride across the bay from the Ship Repair and Port Facility. Only military personnel had to endure the eight-hour bus ride from Clark AFB in the tropical heat of the Philippine Islands. Most of the new arrivals had begun their journeys from Travis AFB more than 36 hours before. The sailors had been allowed a few minutes at Clark to change from dress blues to tropical whites before boarding the bus; the only sleep they had been allowed was in the seat of the C151 cargo plane or on the bus.

A Marine guard entered the bus and checked each person's military ID against his orders before allowing the bus to proceed. After all, there was a war going on only a few hundred miles to the west. This process was completed with the usual military efficiency—the Marine had to give each sailor the obligatory 'hard time.'—"Welcome to the asshole of the world."

"I see you're from Texas, swabby. Only steers and queers come from Texas. Which are you?"

"What the hell is a guy from Kansas doing this far from his Momma?" The usual inter-service ribbing. The sailors did not take the chiding without comment, even though they were dead tired.

"Hey, Marine, what are you doing here without your swab?"

"You sure you know how to read those orders, Corporal? They're written in English!"

"Be careful with that .45, Marine, it might go off accidentally!" It was a traditional greeting between comrades in arms…bluster and braggadocio…definitely a young male response to too much testosterone.

The driver was given directions to the Receiving Barracks (REC-STA) and allowed to proceed through the raised wooden barrier that served as the gate. RECSTA was an old Quonset barracks used to receive new arrivals and provide temporary quarters for those whose permanent duty stations were at sea. Sailors assigned to ships in port were told the berthing location of their assignments and directed to get there on their own hook.

The four sailors assigned to the USS Tunny gathered their gear and hailed a base cab. Filipino civilians, cleared to drive their taxicabs inside the gates of the base, owned the base cabs. These civilian contractors provided a reliable service and were rewarded handsomely relative to the average income for other Filipino nationals. The problem that immediately confronted the four new Tunny sailors was one of communication. The cab driver spoke Tagalog and some broken English. He could not read the written directions from the RECSTA chief petty officer and he could not understand the jabbering of four Americans all trying to talk at once. Finally, one of the four said, "Rivera Pier, Berth One." The driver responded in the affirmative to that location.

The next problem to confront the four passengers was how to get themselves and their gear into a Datsun cab with the doors closed. Each sailor was larger than the average sized Japanese the car was intended to serve…a couple were well over six feet tall.

Compounding this size problem was the amount of gear each sailor was obliged to carry to their new duty stations. In addition to a regulation seabag filled to capacity and weighing about 100 pounds, each sailor carried a duffle filled with personal gear intended for use during travel. However, once the Datsun's trunk was lashed down with some packing twine, the four young men squeezed into the cab, three in back, and one in front with the driver. The small frame of the driver forced him to position the front seat as close to the dashboard as possible. The front seat passenger and the poor fellow in the back over the drive shaft hump were forced to ride the last mile and a half to their final destination with their knees covering their ears.

Meanwhile, at Berth One, Rivera Pier, aboard the USS Tunny, the watch was changing. Aboard US Navy ships, the duty day is broken up into four-hour time periods. Each time period is a duty watch and is signaled, on larger vessels, with the sounding of the ship's bell. At eight bells, the watch is changed and new personnel take their duty stations. However, aboard Tunny, a diesel-electric submarine of WWII vintage, no bells were sounded. The watch was changed silently, but routinely, just as it had been ever since the Tunny was commissioned in 1943. While the sailors who served in Tunny could rotate duty watches and even duty sections, the boat itself was never off duty. She was constantly vigilant and the sailors in the duty section made sure she was ready for sea at any moment.

ENFN Jim Woods had just taken the topside watch. His first official task was to make the topside duty log entry. It read as follows:

> "2400 hours, 26Dec1966. Aboard USS Tunny, APSS 282, moored port side to Berth One, Rivera Pier, Subic Bay Naval Station, Republic of the Philippines. Four lines down and doubled. Taking electric and water service from the pier. Duty section two in service with LTJG. Oldham as Duty Officer. MM2 (SS) Rance on below decks watch. Tunny ashore. ENFN Woods on topside watch. All's well topside."

Woods closed the logbook and withdrew the .45 automatic from the duty belt. He manually operated the pistol's mechanism to ascertain that it was not loaded and in working order. Once sure he was in possession of an operable weapon, he toured the topside deck of Tunny, checking each mooring line and utility service entrance to make certain that none were in a bind as a result of the changing tide.

The teakwood deck of Tunny was slick with the evening dew. The temperature was still well over 70 degrees F and the humidity over 90%. At this latitude in December, a pleasant evening. Woods returned to the foredeck and surveyed the gangway as a precaution that the changing tide had not loosened it from its moorings. The tide was out and the deck of Tunny was about five feet lower than the pier. Jim climbed the gangway to inspect its dockside moorings. He adjusted the lines that secured the gangway to the bollard and guardrail on the pier. Once this was complete, he returned to the watch box and retrieved a pack of Marlboros, popped a cigarette from the pack, pulled out his brand new Zippo lighter and lit up. He relaxed against the sail of Tunny to smoke his cigarette.

"Another fucking midwatch!" he thought. "Why me? I always draw the shit duty! I won't hit the sack until 0430 and then reveille is at 0700. At least it's Christmas and we're on light duty." His thoughts turned to his last liberty the previous night. On Christmas evening, Tunny had thrown the crew a party at the CPO Club. There had been barbequed something, baked potatoes, fresh salad (a real treat for West Pac sailors whose bodies craved vitamin C) and ice cream and cake for dessert. The COB (Chief of the Boat—ranking enlisted man) had played Santa and everyone had gotten something. All the smokers had gotten new Zippo lighters with the ship's patch engraved on the front. Non-smokers had been given money clips with the same emblem attached to an Eisenhower silver dollar. Woods couldn't help but smile when he thought of the silver dollar money clips. Most of the guys had taken them over to Olongapo that night and traded them for a piece of ass. No one could trade the crappy Zippo lighter for anything!

Woods was still chuckling to himself when lights of an approaching car shined directly into his eyes as it turned onto the pier. He shielded them with his hand and walked to the gangway to investigate. The base cab pulled up next to the gangway and stopped. Four white-clad sailors emerged from the Datsun's interior and thankfully stretched cramped muscles. One sailor produced a pocketknife and cut the packing twine that was used to lash the trunk lid shut.

"Is this the Tunny?" came the query from the pier.

"Yeah! Who's askin'" said Woods.

"We got orders to report here. Permission to come aboard."

Woods replied, "Leave your gear on the pier and bring your orders down here so I can look at 'em. Permission to board granted." The cab driver was paid and the gear stacked on the pier.

It was necessary for the new Tunny sailors to grab the wire rope handrail as they clambered down the gangway. Their leather-soled shoes combined with the dew-moistened and highly inclined gangway made the trip aboard treacherous. As each sailor reached the deck of Tunny, they saluted the colors aft and then saluted Woods. They were greeted with the obligatory salutation of "Welcome aboard."

Once more their orders were checked against their military IDs, this time by Woods. With all the formalities completed, including a topside log entry which noted each sailor's name, rank, serial number and time of arrival, two sailors went back ashore to retrieve their gear. Woods' log entry read:

> "0030—Reporting for duty were: SA Burris T. Lang, B300956; FA Simon G. Berg, B300215; FN David P. Jackson, B301018 and SN Roger R. Roads, B300823. All orders inspected and verified. New arrivals referred to Duty Officer for assignment."

Woods then walked to a door in the starboard side of Tunny's sail and pulled the sound powered phone from its bracket. He dialed in the control room and turned the crank on the side of the phone bracket. A perceptible squawk was produced from the phone in the Control Room immediately below. Rance, the below decks watch, lifted the receiver, pushed the button on the handset and said, "Control!"

Speaking into his handset, Woods said, "Eddie, this is topside. I got fresh meat coming aboard."

"Take them to the AB hatch and send 'em down. I'll wake the Duty Officer."

"You got it," said Woods.

The seabags were tossed aboard and each sailor gathered his

personal gear. More observant than the others, Fireman Jackson asked, "What the hell's that bubble lookin' thing back there?"

"That's the hangar. Tunny used to be a Regulus missile boat. The hangar has been converted to carry troops and UDT. We do special ops in 'Nam." said Woods.

"Who the hell are UDT and what do you mean by special ops?" queried Roads.

"You'll find out soon enough. For now, let's get your orders to the Duty Officer and get your gear stowed." Woods led the way aft along the outboard side of the sail to the after battery hatch. A circular opening in the deck emitted a light that indicated life below decks.

Woods took each seabag to the hatch and yelled, "Look out below—Watch your heads!" He proceeded to drop each seabag the twelve feet down onto the After Battery mess deck.

"Hey!" yelled Berg, "I got some breakable stuff in there!"

"Well, non-qual, it's unbreakable for fuckin' sure now," came the reply from below. Eddie Rance was pulling the seabags aside as fast as Jim Woods dropped them through the hatch.

"Shit! My whole seabag's gonna smell like English Leather!" said Berg.

"You done droppin' shit from up there!" yelled Eddie.

"One more! Comin' down!" Woods dropped the last bag through the hatch. There was an unmistakable sound of breaking glass from the mess deck.

"Which one of you dipshits packed fufu juice in your seabag?" This was a new voice. The irritated Duty Officer, LTJG Oscar Oldham, had been aroused from his night's rest to greet the new Tunny sailors. He was already irritated because he had to take duty during the Christmas holiday, but now to be awaked by new non-qualified arrivals really went too far.

"Get the fuck down here and clean this mess up! Rance, send these idiots to the wardroom with their orders when they get below decks, yelled Oldham."

"Aye, sir," said Eddie.

Berg was the first to attempt the descent into the bowels of Tunny. He leaned over, found the topmost rung on the ladder with his right foot and began to let himself down. About three rungs down, he got hung up. He had wedged his knee and backside between the ladder and the back of the hatchway. He could neither go up nor down and his body weight was beginning to put excruciating pressure on his knee.

"Yooooow! How do I get out of this damn trap?" squealed Simon.

"Jesus Christ! These guys are so stupid they can't even come down a ladder!" Eddie climbed up the ladder, placed his hand under Simon's butt and pushed him back up the ladder, which freed him from his entrapment.

"Look, dumb ass! Turn your legs sideways…like this. This ain't no whorehouse you're comin' into." Eddie demonstrated the proper technique for descending submarine ladders. By twisting his lower body sideways, he had plenty of room to negotiate the cramped hatchway. Later, with more experience, the sailors would quickly learn to grab the sides of the ladder and drop straight down without the use of the ladder rungs at all.

"Is this some kind of initiation?" said Seaman Apprentice Lang.

"Brother, it's just the beginning!" replied Woods.

Once assembled in the After Battery, Eddie led the new recruits forward through the Control room to the Forward Battery compartment and into the wardroom. There sat LTJG Oldham with the ship's log. He took each new shipmate's orders, made the appropriate log entries and stood to face the "fresh meat" who had been at attention the entire time.

"At ease. Welcome to Tunny, men. I'm sure you didn't deliberately disturb my beauty rest and we can sure use the new manpower. Right now, you'll be assigned bunks in the hangar where you can stow your gear. Petty Officer Rance will show you how to get there. Quarters is at oh eight hundred, so get some rest. If you're hungry, Rance will show you around the galley. Just clean up after yourselves. Report to me first thing after quarters in the morning. You got all that?"

"Yes, sir. Aye, Aye sir!" was the simultaneous reply.

The four bewildered new recruits stumbled out of the wardroom and retraced their steps to the crew's mess deck in the After Battery compartment. Rance gave them a quick tour of the galley. He cautioned them once more against leaving a mess for someone else to clean up. Then he led them further aft to the ladder that led up to the hangar deck.

It was exactly the same size and construction as the ladder they had descended into the After Battery. Only this time they had to ascend through the narrow opening. Jackson was the largest of the new Tunny sailors, standing three inches over six feet. Even by contorting his lower body it was difficult for him to manage the climb up into the hangar—especially with his 100 lb. seabag balanced on his head. The others didn't have as difficult a time, but all emerged in the dim light of the hangar with a healthy covering of perspiration on their bodies and grease on their white uniforms.

They placed their belongings in the middle of the hangar deck as Rance switched on the lights. There, behind them, was the huge hangar door standing open to the fantail. And looking at them through an opening sixteen feet in diameter was Jim Woods, the topside watch. Woods and Rance both had wry smiles on their faces. The new guys had just hauled their 100 pounds of gear down to the mess deck and then back up to the hangar deck—a completely unnecessary journey. They stood less than 15 yards from the gangway and could reach out their hands and touch the dock. They had fallen victim to their first prank—the Tunny obstacle course.

Chapter Two

Sanitary

Jackson awoke to reveille being played over the 1MC. It took him a few minutes to orient himself. He had been dreaming—of what he could not remember—so reveille had interrupted a particularly deep slumber. His chosen 'rack' was not long enough to accommodate his 185 lb., 6'3" frame. Consequently, his legs hung off the end of his bunk from his ankles down. They had left the huge hangar door open all night for natural ventilation, but the sun had been up for two hours and it was turning the steel hangar compartment into an oven. He had slept in his GI skivvies but his entire body and bedding were soaked in his own sweat. Jackson took a few seconds to survey his surroundings.

They were quite different from his home on the eastern plains of Wyoming. His father was employed at a large open-pit coalmine. They were decidedly a middle class family and his youth had been the usual small town America existence. His mother had given birth to three children—he was the oldest—and they had all attended the same local schools in Gillette. His father's job was stable and had not involved any relocation since their settling in Gillette. David Jackson, Sr. was a graduate of the Colorado School of Mines and had completed his education on the GI Bill of Rights for WWII veterans. The only occasion the Jackson children had to leave Gillette, Wyoming had been their annual two-week vacations. Most of these had been spent with their grandparents in Cheyenne or Laramie.

David had spent his teenage summers on his maternal grandfather's cattle ranch just north of Laramie. He had learned to 'cowboy' at an early age and the profession no longer held any mystery for him. However, his grandfather had employed a ranchhand everyone called 'Sailor George.' At night, after the daily work was complete and supper had been devoured, George would regale his fellow ranch hands with tales of the Far East—of such exotic places as Tahiti and Hong Kong and the winsome women that lived there. George would tell of warm nights on white sand beaches, swimming in clear blue waters with naked, compliant, beautiful girls whose only wish in life was to please the 'round-eyed' sailors. David would fall asleep with these whimsical pictures dancing in his imagination as the far off sound of a train whistle came through the open window of his room in his grandparent's two-story house.

After graduating from high school, David followed his father's footsteps to the Colorado School of Mines in Golden, Colorado. Golden is located just outside of Denver and is the home of Coors Brewery. Denver, Coors and a beautiful flaxen-haired coed named Patsy had consumed David's interests. At the end of the second semester at Mines, David's grades were not passing and his academic career was placed on probation. Patsy began dating one of his fraternity brothers and David returned to Gillette to work as a day laborer in the mine.

One bitterly cold day that winter, a letter of greetings arrived at the Jackson home with an invitation for David to report to Cheyenne for his pre-induction physical at the expense of his Uncle Sam. He was informed that, upon passing this physical exam, he would receive his draft notice within two weeks.

While in Cheyenne at the recruiting depot, David caught sight of a Navy chief petty officer sitting in his office. Behind the Chief, on the wall of his office, was a large poster of Hawaii. On the poster, the sun was setting into a black sea behind a single coconut palm while a girl in a grass skirt danced the hula on the beach. David joined the Navy immediately. While at boot camp, he volunteered for submarine duty and was accepted. He had just spent three months in New London, Connecticut at basic submarine school.

The Navy was very particular about who they let ride in their submersible fleet. Basic aptitude and IQ tests were combined with a psychological battery of tests to determine each sailor's resistance to claustrophobia and any other "phobia." Because of the missions assigned to submarines and the equipment issued to complete such assignments, all sub sailors had to obtain a security classification of at least a "secret" level. As a matter of policy, no one in the US Navy who was even suspected of homosexuality could be issued a secret security clearance.

While at sub school, several students washed out for academic failures, others for the lack of physical ability and others for mysterious failings not quite clear to their classmates. Sailors would get called from class and never return. That evening in the barracks, their bunks were rolled up and they had disappeared as if they had never existed. Questions as to their whereabouts were answered with vague comments about reassignment and it was made obvious that such questions were not appreciated.

David now lay three bunks up from the hangar deck on a piece of canvas lashed to a metal frame which was attached to the bulkhead with hinges and sway braced at both ends. The smell of English Leather from Simon's seabag had overpowered the ever-present smell of diesel fuel in the hangar.

Submarines of Tunny's vintage were nothing more than floating fuel drums. Saddle tanks filled with diesel fuel surrounded the pressure hull, providing the boat with a capacity of almost 100,000 gallons of highly aromatic diesel fuel. That much of the volatile liquid meant that everything on board smelled like diesel fuel—everything—except Berg's seabag and the hangar on this particular morning.

Jackson grabbed the bunk above him with his left hand, lifted himself to the edge of his bunk and threw his left leg over and down. He had placed his foot directly onto Simon Berg's crotch sleeping in the bunk directly beneath.

"What the shit!" yelled Simon? "I'm awake! You don't have to kick me in the nuts!"

"Sorry, Simon. What the hell are you doing with a woodie?" inquired David.

"I've had to pee since 0300, but I'm afraid to climb down from here in the dark. What's that weird looking thing back aft, next to the hatch?" asked Simon.

"How the fuck am I supposed to know! It looks like a giant spider from here!" replied David. In fact it was the pneumatic and hydraulic mechanism that operated the huge hangar door and elevated the deck and railway that led to the fantail. They would quickly learn not only how to operate the door and deck, but they would have to trace all the pneumatic and hydraulic oil piping back to the fluid source.

"That's what I thought, too," said Simon. "I've kept my eye on it all night—afraid that it would attack me when I fell asleep. I've heard about giant spiders in the Philippines and that looked like one to me!"

"Christ, Simon, are you that big a candy-ass!" It was Burris Lang. He was in the bunk above David. He was attempting to free himself from his confinement between his sleeping space and the overhead.

"Shit!" His accent was unmistakable—the high-pitched nasal tones of his East Texas twang resonated off the steel bulkheads. The word "Shit" came out as "She-It."

"Ya have to climb out of this damn rack just to change your mind!"

They all laughed and began their careful descent to the hangar deck. They gathered their clean dungarees and douche bags (Navy for shaving kits) and headed for the after battery head. They descended the ladder; this time with some practiced skill, and immediately ran into the queue for the shower.

"Who the crap are you guys?" It was a chief petty officer asking. They could tell because he was wearing his khaki campaign hat and an off the shoulder smile—nothing else. He was also heavily tattooed, some obviously older than others. "And what the fuck are you doing on my boat?"

"Mornin', Chief. My name's David Jackson. Me and Simon and Burris and Roger reported aboard just last night." David stuck out his hand in the universal gesture of salutation.

"What you goin' to do with that hand, Sailor? Give me a hand job?"

The Chief's remark drew a laugh from everyone in the shower line except for David. His face turned beet red as he quickly withdrew his hand and made it into a clenched fist.

"Take it easy, Dave! The Chief's just bull shittin'!" It was Roger Roads, who was the last one down from the hangar.

"You a hothead, sailor?" said the Chief. "You look big enough to hunt Charlie with a slingshot! Just move to the back of the line and keep your skivvies out of your crack!"

"Hey, Chief, where's the head? I have to piss like a dragon." Simon was doing the peepee dance and holding his scrotum at the same time.

"Right there on the starboard side." The Chief pointed to a set of two louvered doors just forward of the hangar deck ladder. "But you can't use 'em right now. The Cook's blowin' sanitaries and the tank's under pressure. Why do ya think we're standin' in this fuckin' line!?"

Normally, a submarine's sanitary tanks are evacuated routinely at the beginning of the morning watch—0400 hours. Because submarines are designed for submerged operations, toilets, sinks, showers and other water waste basins are discharged into a sanitary tank—a quaint oxymoron peculiar only to submarines. The sanitary tank is vented to the interior of the boat so that when it was evacuated outside the pressure hull, all waste drains and vent valves must be shut. Once the tank was under 15 pounds per square inch (PSI) of pressure, the hull valve was opened to allow the sewage to be discharged to sea. This particular morning, someone neglected to 'blow sanitaries' on the morning watch. Hence the queue for the showers.

"But Chief, I gotta pee real bad!" squeaked Simon.

"Go topside and hang it off the starboard side. Don't pee off the port side 'cause you'll be peein' on the pier."

Simon scrambled up the hangar compartment ladder like a man possessed.

"'Scuse me, Chief." It was Roger. He was fast on Simon's heels. Burris and David stood fast. They both had to urinate, but they had already drawn the crew's derision once and they weren't going to be humiliated again if they could help it.

Presently, they could hear the sound of water and high-pressure air escaping from the pressure hull. The duty commissaryman had opened the sanitary tank hull valve to purge the tank to sea. Behind Burris' head was an air gauge that registered a steady 15 psi. This gauge relayed the air pressure in the tank. After about three or four minutes, the pressure gauge reading began to retreat toward zero.

"That means the shit's out of sanitary and in our lovely harbor," said the Chief. "Don't go swimmin' till after lunch, boys." This remark drew another all hands chuckle.

Burris was watching the air pressure gauge. "Chief! The gauge has stopped at five pounds."

"It won't stay there long." The Chief had a mischievous grin on his face.

A small sailor dressed in dungarees, wearing a large white apron that reached to his ankles stepped from behind the shower room bulkhead. He had not been visible before, but it was obvious that he was the duty cook.

"Make a hole." He motioned to Burris as he reached for a small valve below the pressure gauge. He turned it in a counter clockwise direction and pressurized air hissed from the vent line below the deck plates in the battery well. Almost immediately, the smell of human waste permeated the shower space and the sanitary tank pressure gauge fell to zero.

"God, men, don't that smell remind ya of liberty in Olongapo!" The Chief drew a deep breath through his nostrils. Burris and David turned and, with haste, escaped the after battery toward the more familiar surroundings of the hangar. Laughter followed them up the ladder.

They quickly went out on the after deck through the hangar door and headed forward on the starboard side of the hangar. There stood Simon and Roger, urinating into Subic Bay. "I don't think it will hurt anything," said Roger. "We just saw a whole bunch of shit surface from under the boat a minute ago!"

He and Simon were standing on Tunny's main deck—a full six-feet from the waterline.

Simon was holding his penis in his left hand and grinning in relief as the contents of his bladder mixed with the discharge from the sanitary tank. "Boy, that water's cold!" laughed Simon.

"Yeah!" said Roger with a sigh of relief; "and deep too!"

Chapter Three

Quarters

It was two days after Christmas and a workday for all hands. The entire crew would be aboard for quarters at 0800. Lieutenant Commander William C. Browne leaned over to kiss his wife, Emily, goodbye. She would need the car to go to the Base Exchange that day. Some Christmas gifts had to be exchanged, especially the revealing peignoir she had received from Bill. He still saw her as his own pinup girl, even after all these years.

He brushed her lips with his and reached across to pat his son on the head. Bill, Jr. was 18 months old. He'd been born in Charleston, South Carolina while Bill had been on sea trials with the USS Chopper out of Key West. Somehow the message that Emily's labor had started hadn't reached the Chopper in time for him to take leave for the birth of his son. He suspected that Commander Wright, the Chopper's skipper, had withheld the message until they were underway. He would never forgive Wright for that.

"Come get me around seventeen hundred hours, Baby. I'll be done by then."

"Bill, you know I don't know what that means! Can't you speak English when we're alone?" Emily Browne was deeply in love with her husband, but she refused to submit to military time and regulations. It was her small rebellion against a life that had taken her all over the world for the last seventeen years. She had set up housekeeping on so many bases in so many tank towns that they had all begun to look alike. Just when she got familiar with her surroundings, they were transferred and had to start over again.

Fortunately, Navy wives were a small sorority. The families eventually ended up in all the same places, so one would run into them again and again—only the base name would change. They had a cadre of close friends, so acquaintances were often renewed many times over.

This was Bill's first assignment outside the continental US. Oh, there had been that terrible year in Alaska right after he had graduated from Annapolis. But they had been so in love then, that even the midnight sun could not dampen their ardor. This was also Bill's first command. He had earned it after seventeen years of almost constant sea duty.

"Alright, Baby. Be here at five o'clock this afternoon—with the car, please!" teased Bill. He smiled and spun on his heel, heading for the Tunny's gangway.

"Hey, sailor!" Emily yelled after him, "Did you have a good time last night?"

This had been her ritual farewell for years. He had long since come to expect it and, so, was no longer embarrassed by it. But he laughed anyway and waved over his shoulder.

About this time he spotted four young sailors in their GI skivvies ducking back into the hangar from the starboard side of Tunny's sail. He didn't recognize any of them. Bill knew every member of his crew on sight. He also knew the wives of those who were married. He had been expecting new crew at any time. Tunny was shorthanded and at sea some of the crew had been on "port and starboard" watches. This usually meant six hours on watch followed by six hours off. After a couple of weeks of this monotony, the crew was exhausted and morale began to fall. New crew meant the end to port and starboard as soon as he could get these new sailors qualified on their assigned watch duties.

As he reached the pier side of the gangway, the topside watch spoke into the 1MC, "Tunny—arriving." The tide had come in with the sunrise and the gangway was almost horizontal to the deck.

Bill saluted the colors aft and returned the salute of the topside watch who was, standing at rigid attention.

"Carry on," Bill said and walked forward to the forward torpedo room companionway. He descended into the forward torpedo room through the escape trunk.

The escape trunk was normally a useless space on most submarines. With very few exceptions, when submarines are lost at sea they are lost in water so deep that escape would be hopeless even if the pressure hull remained in tact. But on Tunny, the forward escape trunk got plenty of use and was an integral part of their mission.

LCDR Browne stood 5' 11" tall and weighed 165 lbs. He had a full head of thick brown hair and brown eyes. His countenance and bearing displayed confidence in himself and in those that were privileged to serve with him. To a man, he had earned the respect and admiration of his officers and crew. This leadership quality is imperative on a Navy Man-o-War that was regularly in harm's way. To say that his crew would follow him through the fires of hell had already been proven as an understatement.

Browne ducked through the watertight door between the forward torpedo room and the forward battery and turned into the wardroom on the port side. LTJG. Oldham, eating his breakfast at the wardroom table, rose to his feet when the Captain of the Tunny entered. "Morning, Sir" said Oscar Oldham.

"Mornin', Oscar. Take your seat and finish your breakfast. I see we have new crew members today."

"Yessir. They reported last night." Oldham was surprised at this revelation from the Skipper. How did the Old Man know about the new sailors? He had been ashore when they reported in! Was he clairvoyant? Oscar, of course, thought the Old Man walked on water anyway.

"I'd like to meet them after COB has given them their watch-quarter-station assignments. Tell COB to have them report to me at his earliest convenience," Browne said.

All new crew members on all Navy ships and shore stations had billets assigned on the watch-quarter-station bill. On surface vessels, the first thirty days were usually spent in the galley as mess cooks. But on subs, there was only room for one, maybe two, mess cooks at a time in the galley. So new men were routinely assigned to the deck gang until they designated a rate (job) for which they wished to strike. They then became a "striker" or beginner under training for that job specialty.

Submarines, unlike surface vessels, are called "boats" instead of "ships." This tradition in the submarine Navy is derived from the early days of the silent service when the small submersible crafts could be lifted aboard a tender for maintenance. Hence, they were boats. It had been years and many technical evolutions since submarines could be winched onto the sub tender, but the tradition had stuck. And those that served them in were "boat sailors." They shared a special bond that few people would ever know, for their lives depended everyday upon the training and bravery of each of their shipmates. One careless mistake could send all hands to Davey Jones' locker.

The Chief of the Boat (COB) was the ranking enlisted man. His duties were to supervise the other enlisted personnel in their assignments and training. In submarines because of the constant danger, training was intensive and thorough. Each crewmember knew the entire physical layout and construction of Tunny. They knew the location and purpose of every valve, pipeline, switch, and electrical connection. In the event that one shipmate was unable to perform his assigned duty, another qualified sub sailor could complete the work with little loss of efficiency. So on submarines, qualified sailors could load torpedoes or operate the stern planes or stand watch in maneuvering with almost equal skill. From the Captain to the mess cook, if they had earned their dolphins, they knew each other's jobs. And there was the caveat—if they had earned their dolphins by completing qualifications!

The COB supervised this training of all new hands. Qualifications took anywhere from six months to a year—depending upon ones rank. Each air system, each hydraulic system, each fuel system, each electrical system, etc. had to be mastered and proficiency in its operation had to be demonstrated. A submariner's dolphins are as sacred to him as an aviator's wings are to a flyer. And once the dolphins are earned, they are worn with just as much pride.

Topside, the crew was forming up to quarters. Each morning at 0800, the crew assembled in formation by division on the forward deck. The division chiefs reported to the division officers who in turn reported to the Executive Officer (XO). On this particular day, LTJG Oscar Oldham was Duty Officer, and as such, was standing in for the XO. He stood facing the Tunny crew to receive reports. No one was unaccounted for, but several were on leave as it was the Christmas holiday. Tunny had been promised the holidays off as a reward for some recently successful special operations along the coast of Vietnam. She would return to 'Nam again soon and Captain Browne wanted his men rested and alert for the next evolution.

The COB and LTJG Oldham conferred briefly while the crew remained in formation. Master Chief Petty Officer Ronald Vincent was the Tunny's COB. Chief Vincent had already met the new swabbies in the shower room earlier that morning. He relayed that information to Oldham and got the Captain's request from Oscar to see the new men upon completion of assignments.

Vincent executed a military about-face to confront the crew's formation and yelled, "Atten-shun! Fall out! Roads, Jackson, Berg, and Lang—front and center!"

David, Simon, Roger and Burris hustled to face the COB. Each stood at attention and awaited assignment. Suddenly, all four of their mouths went slack as the COB stood in front of them. Here was the naked chief they had met earlier that morning in the after battery shower room! David was immediately embarrassed and tried to apologize,

"Ah, Chief, ah, sorry 'bout this morning...I..."

"Forget it, sailor. Just keep your fuckin' cool from now on...you'll need it!" said the COB. "Now listen up. Jackson, you and Berg are in Duty Section Three. They're the most short-handed. All your watch-quarter-station assignments will be posted by section. That goes for all you non-quals. Roads, you're assigned to section two and Lang, you go to section one. Three has duty today. Until you get qualified to stand watches alone, you will be assigned to stand watches with a qualified individual. Check the duty roster everyday before quarters for your duty assignments. By quarters tomorrow you will be assigned a 'sea daddy' who will help you with orientation and quals. Go to him with your questions and problems. One last thing—and this is very fuckin' important—don't flip any switches, operate any valves or open any doors or hatches until you have been checked out and qualified as an operator. One stupid mistake can take this old lady to the bottom—so until you're qualified don't touch nothin'—got it?"

Chief Vincent handed each new Tunny sailor an 8½"x11" laminated cardboard form. "This is your qualifications card. You are expected to learn and be tested orally on each system on Tunny. This process should not take longer than six months. Failure to complete the quals process in that time will earn you a one-way ticket to the skimmer Navy. Right now you are all in the deck gang until otherwise assigned. See Chief Keller—the skinny guy right over there"— Vincent pointed to a lanky fellow standing forward of the capstan wearing regulation blue dungarees and a Chief's hat—"and he'll tell you what to do while we're in port. Any questions?"

Burris raised his hand, "OK, non-qual. Speak!" said COB.

"Chief, what's a non-qual?" asked Burris.

"You stupid shit! That's you, numb nuts—and anyone else in the whole wide fuckin' world that hasn't earned his dolphins! You earn your dolphins by finishing the work on that quals card I just gave you! Any more stupid fuckin' questions?" Vincent shouted.

Fully intimidated by this time, none of the four new "non-quals" wanted to hang around with COB to ask the myriad of questions that ran through their minds.

"OK then, let's get your asses to work. Chief Keller!" COB shouted. Keller turned to face COB and acknowledged his call. Keller finished some last minute instructions to one of his deck hands and then joined the group with Chief Vincent.

"What's up, COB?" queried Keller.

"These new non-quals are assigned to your deck crew as of today. Put them to work and see to it that they don't sink this old tub in the process. Got it?"

"Aye, Chief. I got just the job for 'fresh meat'." A sly smile crept over Keller's face. "Follow me, gentlemen."

With that they were led to an open hatch in the free-flooding superstructure on Tunny's forward deck. Keller handed each new sailor a wire brush and a chipping hammer.

"Climb in there and chip the old paint off the hull. I want it down to bare metal by liberty call. Which one of you shit-birds is in section three?" David and Simon raised their hands. "Finally," said Keller, "some relief. Three has duty today. I'm the duty Chief, so I'll be assigning duty watches for you guys. I'll want each of you on watch topside tonight with a trainer. I want you two qualified on topside watch by the next in-port duty day so you can stand your own damn watches. Got it!?"

"Aye, Chief!" said David and Simon.

"OK, now get to work."

Crawling into the superstructure of a Gato class submarine is not an easy proposition. The space was cramped and filled with bulkheads and structural members that supported Tunny's main weather deck. This superstructure is welded to the pressure hull to give the fleet boats their distinctive silhouette. Unfortunately, the constant movement of any steel vessel through seawater gives rise to a process of electrolysis. Some of this natural corrosion process is offset by the placement of hull-mounted bars of zinc. The zincs act as sacrificial anodes to ameliorate the damage to the steel ship's hull members. But the zincs were not entirely successful. So, to further protect the ship's hull, liberal applications of paint are used. The old layers of paint had to be removed to allow adhesion of the new applications. This hull maintenance assignment is the responsibility of the deck gang. On surface vessels, the deck gang was usually seaman supervised by Boatswain's Mates. On submarines, the deck gang was composed of all non-qual seaman from the torpedo gang. Chief Keller was the leading Torpedoman in Tunny. So, consequently hull maintenance fell to him and his crew. David, Roger, Simon and Burris were now officially deck gang members.

As they crawled around in the superstructure removing old paint with the wire brushes and chipping hammers, the day began to warm. Airflow was restricted in the superstructure and the sun was beginning to heat the steel surroundings. Add to this the exertion required to complete the work assignment and it became clear why the "fresh meat" was given this intolerable task. After an hour at work, their dungarees were soaked with sweat and filthy with paint chips and rust. Saddle tanks surrounded the pressure hull of Tunny. Saddle tanks were used for ballast and fluid storage. The tank tops were only exposed within the superstructure. These tank tops collected water that had to be removed before paint could be applied. Part of their job was to scoop the water from the tank tops and this involved the inevitable dousing with stagnant, smelly salt water. From personal experience, Keller knew that he had to see to it the new sailors had relief every hour or they would lapse into heat exhaustion.

"Non-quals!," yelled Keller. "Report topside immediately!"

To their relief, they scrambled to the hatch and the cooler air on deck. (It was well over 90 degrees at 0930.)

"What are your names? I can't keep calling your guys by number," Keller asked.

"David Jackson, Chief."

"Simon Berg,"

"Roger Roads, Chief"

"Burris Lang," said Burris.

"What the fuck kinda name is Burris? I ain't gonna go 'round callin' one o' my hands Burris! Don't ya got a better name, son? Burris sounds like a piano player in a whorehouse!" said Keller.

"Well, Chief, my middle name is Timothy—after my Grandpa." said Burris in his East Texas accent.

"From now on you're 'Tim', got it? That's better anyway—I got a nephew named Timmy. Ain't seen the little tyke in 10 years, though. He's my sister's kid and lives in Louisville.

"You swabs get some water and take a 10-minute breather. Then get back at it. Tim, I'm puttin' you in charge o' this detail. Make sure everyone gets a break every hour and make sure ya'll get plenty o' water. Noon meal is served for our crew at 1130 hours—be there or you'll miss chow. Got that, sailor?" ordered Keller.

Burris—now Tim to all Tunny sailors—seemed to grow a couple of inches and his face beamed in a big East Texas smile. He was suddenly Chief Keller's most loyal follower and Keller had replaced Mickey Mantle as his idol.

"You bet, Chief." said Tim in his most forceful voice. He watched Keller proceed forward to assist maintenance on the line lockers.

"You guys heard the Chief! Get a drink and cool off for a few," repeated Tim.

"Brown-noser," said Simon.

"Suck-up," said Roger.

David made a circle out of his right index finger and thumb and began making kissing noises with his lips stuck out of the circle. "Ass-kisser," said David.

They all burst into laughter at the same time. For the first time since boarding Tunny, someone had made them feel like belonged here.

Chapter Four

Chow

At 1130 sharp, Simon and David were washed up and in the chow line in the after battery compartment. The smell of hot food was intoxicating. Breakfast had been a surprise to them after Navy mess halls in New London and San Diego. The eggs were prepared to order, pork chops and/or steak were available and there was plenty of fresh fruit. Breakfast was served for anyone on board at the time—usually just the duty section. The other two-thirds of the crew were on liberty until 0800 when quarters was called. But some early arrivals were always present; others chose to sleep in, exhausted from a night's revelry in Olongapo.

The noon meal while in port was always an all-hands evolution. The small space in the after battery mess made it impossible to serve the entire crew all at once. There were only five tables bolted to the deck. Benches for seating either lined the bulkhead or were riveted to the deck. These benches served a double duty as they were also used for storage. The crew who were fed in the enlisted mess were cycled through in shifts—the duty section eating first. Therefore, today section three ate between 1130 hours and Noon. Section one took chow at Noon and section two followed last at 1230 hours. Today's menu included spaghetti, meatballs, and fresh lettuce salad. The ever-present apples, oranges, and bananas were on every mess table. The lack of space in the mess area meant that the crew was served family-style. Bowls of spaghetti, sauce and salad were placed on each table as the crew filed in and sat at their prepared places. All Chiefs were first in line and sat at their designated table, but that is where ceremony ceased on submarines.

The noise from the conversation was deafening. Loud voices bounced off the steel bulkheads and overhead. Profanity was casual and prolific. Words that would offend polite society were commonplace. Butter was no longer just butter. It was "the fucking butter" or "the God-Damn salt" or "one of them damn apples." The mess cook's name was interchangeable with such descriptive terms as "asshole", "dip-shit", or "fart-blossom."

Talk centered around the various chores each crew had to complete before the next deployment. Speculation as to the next deployment was very popular. Navy rumors are called "scuttlebutt" and scuttlebutt is a major preoccupation of all sailors. When they are ashore or their ship is in port, conversations centered around when they will again be at sea. When they are at sea, conversations take the opposite turn.

Today, in Tunny, there were four new arrivals to occupy a great deal of the conversation. "I heard one of the guys call himself 'Burris'! Sounds like some kinda farmer to me!" said the messcook.

"Did you see how tall that new Fireman is, Woodsey?" asked a Second Class Machinist's Mate. "Rance said his feet hung off his bunk by six inches!"

"At least," said Jim Woods. "Hey, string-bean," yelled Woods, "What's your name?"

David knew from long experience to whom Woods was talking. "David, but you can call me 'String-bean' awhile longer since you seem to have the shortest fucking memory in Navy history! It was you that signed us in last night, Woodsey!"

"Shit, that's right. I forgot! Will you ever forgive me, String-bean," laughed Woods sardonically.

"Only if you give me your sister's address for when I get back to the world," said David.

"Sure," said Jim, "I gave it to the last non-qual washout and he dropped off a case o' clap with her when he breezed through LA. She said she would save a dose for the next sucker I sent her way."

Sisters, mothers, grandmothers—no one was sacred to these young salts. Part of the initiation process, and indeed part of the qualification process, was to learn to develop a thick skin. Nothing that was said was to be taken personally. But there was a creed among these men—never abandon your post, never let your shipmate down and never let another sailor insult your boat. In time, they would

become closer than blood kin—closer than brothers. Their relationships would transcend years and at gatherings 50 years in the future
they would greet each other as if they had never parted.

The noon repast was also being served in the wardroom. Only
four officers were aboard Tunny on this day. The remaining four
officers were on leave over the Holidays. In addition to the captain
and LTJG Oldham, LT Mike O'Rourke and LT Harvey Turner were
on board.

LT Turner had relieved Oscar as Duty Officer and O'Rourke
was 1st Lieutenant, the designation given to the officer in charge of
deck crews and all torpedo and gunnery operations. Tunny's holiday
paint job required O'Rourke's presence and supervision. Although
Chief Keller was perfectly capable of deck gang supervision,
O'Rourke knew notations on his annual fitness report would be
influenced by the quality and efficiency of this task.

O'Rourke was a "mustang"—the term applied to an officer who
had risen from the enlisted ranks. By reaching the rank of Lieutenant,
O'Rourke felt he had reached the zenith of his Navy advancement.
However, annual fitness reports affected promotions, privileges, and
duty assignments. Assignment to Tunny was a plum for any naval
officer. Tunny was the only submarine in the fleet to regularly see
action in Vietnam. Her configuration for special operations made her
a special ship. With an officer's gold dolphins and Vietnam campaign
ribbons, easy shore duty was almost assured afterwards.

O'Rourke was headed to San Diego when he finished his tour
in Tunny. He had a partnership in a bar on Broadway, purchased
with funds saved and otherwise accumulated over his long career.
His second wife's brother was his partner and was running the place
for him now. But, even though he trusted Paddy not to cheat him,
his second wife was a different story.

Erlene had been a stripper in a club along Pine Street in Seattle
when he met her. He woke up one morning in Bremerton with a
hangover and a ring on his left hand. When he rolled over, there was
Erlene in bed next to him. She had one of the biggest damn diamond rings on her left hand he had ever seen. He had been on a
two-week bender and had spent every dime he had in the world on
Erlene and their whirlwind romance. "Shit," thought Mike, "I don't
even remember fuckin' her!"

Erlene was loyal as long as Mike had money and was in port.

Neither of these things occurred simultaneously. He had returned to Bremerton from a West Pac cruise ten years ago to find their apartment as bare as her stripper's ass. His car had been repossessed and their joint checking account was in overdraft. Erlene was nowhere to be found.

Mike looked up her brother, Paddy Ryan, with the intent of getting his pound of flesh from him. But Paddy was just as mystified as Mike as to Erlene's whereabouts. They formed a friendship over a few beers at the Chief's Club and had been buddies ever since. Erlene eventually turned up, broke and heroin addicted, in Seattle. Part of the divorce settlement had required her to attend Drug and Alcohol dependency treatments. She had given the cure her best attempt, but Paddy was continuously bailing her out of one scrape after another.

Mike felt sorry for Paddy and probably for himself, as well. They corresponded often—really the only family each one had. Paddy had moved to San Diego to work in the National Shipyard there. Mike had been assigned to the USS Trout at Point Loma and he and Paddy hooked up on liberty several times over the next couple of years. In the process, Paddy and Mike became friends with an old Navy retiree who owned a bar on Broadway in downtown Dago. The old salt was weary of the daily demands of the pub and wanted to sell out. However, his asking price was more than Mike could afford. Whereupon a scheme was devised that allowed Mike to buy a half interest in the bar. It was further agreed that Paddy would handle daily operations.

Things went fine until Erlene showed up in Dago two weeks before Mike shipped out for Tunny. She still had a great body and she claimed she was recovering from her addictions—she said she had been clean for two years. She was divorced again and was hiding out from her latest ex-husband who had threatened to kill her. Mike wasn't sure whose side he was on, having been one of Erlene's previous victims. She went to work for Paddy in the bar as a "hostess" and her looks brought in a lot of business from horny First Fleet sailors.

But every time Mike recalled his devastation after their breakup, he had nightmares. He needed to finish this tour in Tunny and get back to Dago in a hurry. Trouble was, duty assignments to ships like

Tunny were for at least one year. Mike would complete his year in few months and the Skipper had guaranteed him a transfer if he could earn excellent marks on his next efficiency report. He knew he was being bribed, but he was a willing participant as long as it got him back stateside quickly.

Mike gobbled his food and quickly stood to depart the wardroom. "I gotta get back topside and check on that paint job," said Mike.

"O'Rourke, hold up a minute," said Bill Browne. "I need to see those new sailors ASAP. COB assigned them to your deck gang. When you get topside, have them report to me at 1330 hours."

"Aye, Sir," replied O'Rourke as he departed.

Mike had been elated with the new arrivals. The extra help meant that he could finish the work on the main weather deck early—an improvement on previous Tunny records. He was a little concerned with the Skipper's interest in the fresh meat. Did he want to reassign them to other duties? That would throw a kink in his plans for the paint job. He was already leaning on Keller harder than he liked to get the job finished ahead of schedule.

As Mike emerged from the escape trunk into the companionway, he came upon one of the new non-quals working in the superstructure. "You one of the new guys that reported last night!" Mike had to shout over the sound of a chipping hammer.

Roger was completely taken by surprise by the voice behind him. He turned to find an officer not 12 inches from his face. In attempting to snap to attention and salute, Roger slammed his head into the underside of Tunny's teakwood main deck. He fell to his knees and was caught by O'Rourke before he landed on his face. Mike pulled him topside and sent below for the Corpsman. Roger was laid out on the deck and given a shot of medicinal brandy. The Corpsman found a large knot on his skull, but no permanent damage.

O'Rourke was still smiling when he and Chief Keller assembled the new Tunny deck hands topside. By this time, they were filthy from head to toe. Once spit-shined boondockers were badly scuffed—shirts and trousers were stained and torn. The combination of sweat and seawater left them without a dry stitch on their bodies.

"You boys get cleaned up and get to the wardroom by 1330 hours to meet the Captain. Get those shoes spit-shined and wear your tropical whites. Now, turn to!" ordered O'Rourke. The four bedraggled sailors saluted Mike, unanimously returned an "Aye, Aye Sir," and headed for the showers. Roger was still rubbing the knot off his head as they disappeared around the sail.

"Just kids," Mike said to Chief Keller as he shook his head in bewilderment. "That's what they're sending us nowadays—kids!"

"Yeah, Mike," said Keller. "They're 'bout the same age as we were when we joined up. But they'll do, anyway."

Mike looked at Keller's face. He was watching his new hands retreat to the showers for their appointment with the Skipper. He looked like a mother hen seeing to the welfare of her chicks. "Chiefs," thought Mike. "They give these kids hell, send them to accomplish impossible tasks, berate and belittle them. But they'd stand in front of a bullet for every one 'em." He followed Keller aft to check on the progress of the paint job.

Chapter Five

Katy Lang

Burris T. Lang was almost 6' tall, but he weighed only about 150 pounds. He kind of liked the new name Keller had given him—Tim. The new name seemed to separate him from the Burris Lang of Paris, Texas. Subic Bay was also a long way from Paris.

Burris' father had worked for the grain elevator company in town. They had not been wealthy, but comfortable. Burris and his sister, Katy, had run the household since their mother had died when he was 10 years old. He and his big sister, who was 14 at the time of their mother's passing, took over the domestic duties of the household. Mabel Lang had expired after a lingering illness of over five years. The doctors had diagnosed the disease as uterine cancer and she had been through several surgeries to remove the growth. Apparently none had been completely successful—they only seemed to prolong her agony. By the time she died in her own bed, everyone in the family was prepared for her passing.

Fred Lang had remarried after two years of being a single parent. Burris and Katy's new stepmother, Jobell Wayne, brought two children of her own into the now enlarged family. Burris had been forced to share his once private room with his new stepbrother. Ansel Wayne, known as "Ans" to the Paris Police Department, was a troublemaker—always looking for a short cut to success. Ans was a senior at Paris High when his mother married Fred Lang. He already had a rap sheet that included several misdemeanors and one felony—grand theft auto. He had been given a suspended sentence for that offense since the stolen car was his uncle's.

Burris' sister, Katy, had to share a room with their new stepsister,

Alice. Alice was nice enough for a ten-year-old kid. She immediately developed a crush on Burris. She followed him everywhere.

Burris was in the gym one day for wrestling practice, when he looked up from the mat to see Alice watching through the skylights in the gym roof. She had followed him to school, climbed a work-man's ladder to the roof and stuck her head through the open sky-light to watch Burris practice. He'd had to call his father at work to come pick her up. Burris suffered embarrassment and ridicule from his junior high classmates when he pointed Alice out to the wrestling coach.

The principal at the elementary school had been searching the town frantically for little Alice when she hadn't shown up on the school bus. Jobell was contacted immediately at the truck stop out on the highway where she worked as a waitress. Rather than head-ing to the school immediately, she'd called Fred at the grain elevator. He'd been forced to drop everything to search for Alice. The time off from work had cost him a day's wages—far more than Jobell made at the truck stop.

One night when Burris, now Tim on the Tunny, was a junior in high school, the Paris police showed up at their house. Alice answered the door and was immediately terrified by the large men in uniform carrying guns and nightsticks. She ran to the kitchen to summon her stepfather. Fred ushered the officers into the parlor and called to Jobell. She was in the bathroom on the second floor getting ready to attend her ladies reading club meeting.

With the family assembled, the officers inquired as to the loca-tion of Ans Wayne. The wounded store clerk at the 7-11 in Mount Pleasant had identified him as one of the gang that held up the store that afternoon. The storeowner had been killed during the robbery and Ans had been caught on the store's video recorder (a new inno-vation at all 7-11 stores) as the shooter.

Ans and his two accomplices had stolen the contents of the cash register and had forced the two clerks to lie on the floor. It would be brought out later at the inquest that Ans, with deliberation, had shot both the owner and the employee in the back while they lay on the floor. The Mount Pleasant police had issued an APB for Ans and his friends and the Paris police were dispatched to the Lang home to look for the perpetrators. Fred and the family told the cops everything they knew and promised to phone if Ans showed up. Jobell was indignant.

"How can that no 'count, low-life son of mine shame me like this. Don't he know I gotta live in this town?" she had said. Jobell returned to the upstairs bathroom to finish her preparations for her ladies' reading club meeting

Alice began to cry. Burris put his lanky arms around her for comfort and Katy hugged them all. Fred shook his head in disbelief, while Ans slipped through the back door and into the kitchen just as soon as he'd seen the cops leave. His pants cuffs were blood-spattered.

"I need yur car, Fred! I gotta split Texas for awhile!" Ans was clearly agitated—his nerves were on edge. His eyes didn't stop moving and the gun in his right hand wouldn't stop shaking. He was only about 5' 7" tall, but he was solidly built and could hold his own with any man, as Burris had discovered during their days as roommates.

"Ans, you gotta give yourself up." Fred was calm as he pleaded with his stepson.

"No way, Old Man. They're gonna frame me for the shootin' and I'll get the gas fer sure!" Ans' eyes began to widen with every word and sweat began to develop on his upper lip.

"Ans, listen," said Fred in measured tones, "give me the gun and let me call the police. It'll go easier on ya if'n ya give yourself up. Just lemme have the gun. Katy, get on the phone to the cops."

Ans quickly raised the .38 revolver and pointed it at Katy. "No ya don't, Sis. Leave that God Damn phone alone!" His words became a high-pitched scream and the blood vessels in his forehead began to enlarge and protrude.

Burris recognized this behavior from several childhood encounters with Ans. He had lost control and was now acting beyond reason or forethought. He had become an animal in those brief seconds that Katy had turned and started toward the phone.

"Oh, Ans, don't be so melodramatic," said Katy with a bit of humor in her voice.

"He ain't kiddin'," yelled Burris.

The pistol exploded the same instant the words left Burris' mouth. The bullet caught Katy in the back of her head and exited through her nose. She was dead when she hit the floor. Blood splattered little Alice and the outline of her body could be seen in the bloodstains on the wall in the corridor leading to the parlor. The bullet, having traveled completely through Katy, missed Alice's head by inches.

Burris had found the cast iron skillet that Katy had used to prepare their supper that evening. He swung it almost involuntarily and caught the pistol as the second round left the chamber. The bullet flew harmlessly into the kitchen wall. On the backhand swing, Burris caught Ans across the face. The blow from the heavy skillet laid Ans' nose across his left cheek. Fred jumped at Ans' right arm and twisted the revolver from his grasp as Burris landed one more blow with the skillet on Ans' left arm. The bone broke just above the elbow and Ans began to scream.

Burris rushed to Katy's fallen form and picked her up. He carried her into the parlor and laid her on the good settee. It would have to be thrown away later—the bloodstains could never be removed no matter how much Jobell tried.

"Alice, go next door and tell the Mr. Davis to call the police." Alice didn't move—she remained frozen to the wall, splattered with Katy's blood. "Move, NOW!" yelled Burris. Somehow Alice pried herself loose and ran out the front door in the direction of the Davis house. Ans was still screaming in the kitchen as Fred held him to the floor.

"My arm, you son of a bitch! You broke my fuckin' arm! I'll kill you for this, you mother fucker!" Ans' face was covered with blood, mucus, and saliva, but his eyes were fierce with hatred.

Burris walked calmly down the hall and picked up the revolver from the kitchen floor where it had fallen. As he put the muzzle of the weapon to Ans' temple, he said, "Your killin' days is over, you cock sucker!"

The reason just two bullets went through Ans' brain was simple. There were only two live shells left in the revolver. But, Burris kept pulling the trigger on the double action weapon, the firing pin smashing down again and again on spent cartridges. After what seemed an eternity, Fred reached over, took his son's hand and gently removed the .38 from his grasp. Burris let the weapon fall and went to the parlor to hold his dead sister until the ambulance arrived.

Jobell had just descended from the upstairs bathroom. "Did I hear somethin'?" she inquired.

It was established at the coroner's inquest that Fred Lang had shot his stepson in self-defense, after wrestling the gun from Ans' grasp. Burris had not really agreed with Fred when he volunteered to confess to the shooting. Fred had simply told the Paris police his version of the shooting when they arrived to investigate. Since Jobell had not seen anything until after Ans was killed, she could neither confirm nor deny Fred's testimony. Burris confirmed Fred's version of the killings because he had been taught never to call his Dad a liar. To testify to the contrary would have been unthinkable to him.

Burris finished his high school career in Paris with a cloud over his head, or so it seemed. He kept hearing people whisper behind his back and look away when their eyes would inadvertently meet.

Two years after the shooting, Fred lost his job at the grain elevator and was forced to move to Houston to work at the grain elevators along the ship channel. Burris, Jobell and Alice moved with him until Jobell ran off with one of the men in her reading club. She left Alice with Fred as his adopted daughter. It was unlikely that Alice would have left Fred anyway. She was now devoted to him as the only real father she had ever known. Besides, she was in love with Burris, and the only contact she had with him was through Fred.

Eventually, Burris had joined the Navy and gone off to boot camp in San Diego. Both Alice and Fred drove all the way to Dago for his boot camp graduation. Alice was then 18 and beautiful. When Burris saw her in the grandstand at his boot camp graduation ceremony, tears came to his eyes. All he could see was the blood stained, scared kid standing in the hall of their home in Paris, Texas—her eyes wide with horror and disbelief. She had just witnessed her stepsister's brutal death at the hands of her own brother. Would he ever be able to erase that memory from his own psyche?

The Navy gave him new surroundings and a different perspective. And now the new name—Tim—not Burris; not the person that had shot his stepbrother in cold blood—a new beginning and new friends that didn't know about his past. Maybe now he could forget.

Chapter Six

The Old Man

The Captain of every US Navy ship that has ever been commissioned has been given the colloquialism "Old Man." There are several peculiar familiarities tossed about by sailors to describe their Captain; Skipper, the Boss, Conn Pilot and many others not suitable for mixed company. But the most common and the one that best described how a crew—from the common seaman to the Executive Officer—felt about their Ship's Captain is "The Old Man." It describes the sense of paternalism attributed to the Captain. He was much more than ship's commander to them; he was God and their Father embodied in one person. His word was gospel and his every gesture took on meaning. He exercised complete power over their lives as long as they served in his ship. Even on liberty or on leave, he could control their lives with a phone call or a telegram.

Some men abused this power they had over their crews. Others ignored it and tried to become a member of the crew—one of the gang. Neither of these approaches was successful when it came to leading men into battle where you may be forced to ask any one of them for a supreme sacrifice—Abraham Lincoln's "last full measure…"

Bill Browne took pride in the crew of Tunny. He knew them all by first name and called them by name on informal occasions. He knew how much they could endure and just how far he could push them before they would break. Because they were a highly trained team, they were like a chain—only as strong as the weakest link. That's why he wanted to meet the new arrivals. He had to get them in his sights and pass judgment on their abilities to perform under pressure. Because of Tunny's mission, pressure was a constant companion and disaster was one careless mistake away.

He'd seen it happen on Chopper. Some non-qual had been flipping switches in Maneuvering—trying to understand the main propulsion system—and had inadvertently shut down the entire ship's AC electric system.

Nothing worked afterwards. Lights went out, gauges displayed unbelievable readings and hull valves that operated from electric-driven hydraulic pumps would not operate. Chopper slid toward the bottom at a steep down angle. Her Forward Room was beyond crush depth before an alert Electrician's Mate threw the main motors into "all back full" without orders from the Conn. This action, in addition to the ordered blow of all ballast tanks, safety and bow buoyancy tanks, allowed Chopper to pull herself to the surface stern first and survive. The Electrician's Mate would have been given a commendation, except he was the sailor on duty when the non-qual had shut down the electric system. Instead, he was given a reprimand and would probably be frozen in rank for the remainder of his Navy career.

Browne wanted no such incidents in Tunny. He had learned many negative lessons from Captain Wright. Browne was determined not to have those mistakes repeated on his watch. His commanding officer on Chopper (CDR Wright) had been a detached commander. He hardly knew his officers, let alone his men.

But Browne had also been witness to the other extreme in commanders—the "buddy-buddy" types that treated the crew as equals and never earned their respect. When the chips were down, the crew's lack of respect and slack attitude would cause them to fail to recognize the seriousness of the orders issued from the wardroom and laugh in the face of authority.

There was a knock on the bulkhead just outside the wardroom door. "Enter," said Bill.

Four freshly showered and shaved non-quals shuffled into the cramped wardroom and tried, as best the low overhead would allow, to stand at attention. The tallest sailor spoke first, "Fireman David Jackson reporting as ordered, sir."

"Fireman Apprentice Simon Berg, reporting as ordered, sir."

"Seaman Roger Roads reporting as ordered, sir."

"Seaman Apprentice Tim Lang reporting as ordered, sir."

"Stand at ease, men and have a seat. I just wanted you to meet with me and get an understanding as to what Tunny's mission is. I know you are aware that the Regulus missile hangar has been converted to crews' quarters. See the Chief of the Boat about berthing assignments.

"Tunny's mission is to infiltrate hostile waters covertly to map enemy troop concentrations or disrupt enemy supply logistics. Most of these missions will occur at night and involve the release of Navy Underwater Demolition Teams from a submerged location while Tunny is sitting on the bottom at 56' depth to keel. Tunny's hull has been specially prepared for bottoming.

"Occasionally, Tunny will perform a surface release of forces larger than the eight-man UDT personnel. You will all receive special training in small arms weaponry and small boat handling in addition to your regular submarine qualifications training. At no time are you to reveal Tunny's mission to anyone—not even your families stateside. To do so will risk the lives of all on board.

"Our next operation is scheduled for early in January. I can't tell you more than that. I presume the COB has briefed you on your watch-quarter-station responsibilities and you have been given your qualifications records by this time?"

They all nodded their heads to the affirmative.

"Good. Now I want all of you to report to the Ship's Yeoman before you leave the Forward Battery. In fact, Berg, Lang, and Roads should complete that report right now while I talk to Jackson alone. I will want to talk to each of you privately before you return to your duties with the deck gang. You three may leave now to see the Yeoman while I talk to Jackson."

Simon, Tim, and Roger stood and filed into the passageway. A short, fair-haired second-class petty officer was waiting for them outside the wardroom.

"Hi, guys. I'm Dan Hennessey, the Ship's Yeoman. Follow me." They walked the few paces to the Ships Office and stood in line waiting their turn to complete their business with the Yeoman. Hennessey asked them to confirm their next of kin and other basic family information. They were each given two sheets of Tunny letterhead and told to sit in the Forward Torpedo room and write home to assure their parents or next of kin that they had arrived safely and were in good health. Then they waited their turns for their interviews with the Old Man.

The purpose of Browne's private interviews was to give him a feel for each new sailor and how they would fit in with the rest of the tightly knit crew. Browne had hand picked his officers and CPO's for this particular boat's mission. The other enlisted personnel had been picked by the CPO's for each of their specialties aboard Tunny. Lately, retirements and duty reassignments had left Tunny short handed.

Browne had sent a special request to New London for replacements to fit his unique needs. The replacements had to be single, have some previous experience with firearms and be in the top 10% of their submarine school class.

Browne was asking for the best of the best. Only the top 10% of Navy recruits got to sub school and, then, only if they volunteered. There were no conscripts on submarines—no draftees. The duty was hazardous and stressful. The Navy could not afford to sacrifice a submarine crew of 70-80 men to a malcontent.

After two hours of interviews, Browne felt he had what he needed. Jackson was a born leader. Studious, independent, and smart; he got the impression that Jackson was interviewing him sometimes during their talk. His questions were insightful and displayed a natural inquisitiveness. Browne also liked the fact that he had experienced some Marine boot camp training while enrolled at the Colorado School of Mines. Jackson was solid.

Berg was also a quick study. He had grown up in Boston, the son of a Jewish diamond merchant. His family could have bought three Tunnys and had change left over. But Simon refused to let this material wealth influence his personal relationships. He cultivated friends like a farmer raised crops; he was determined to build friendships and he was never discouraged by a personal rebuff. Simon was the apple of his mother's eye. His father was eternally proud of his son and thanked God each day for such a child.

In return, Simon gave his unqualified love. His childhood had been idyllic. He attended the best private military school in Massachusetts and excelled in all his subjects. He had never found difficulty in any undertaking he attempted. Herein, Browne found a problem. How would Simon react in the face of true adversity—when he was faced with a problem his quick mind could not entirely surround? Browne had a feeling Simon would attack it with the same determination he had everything else in his brief life.

Burris Lang presented the Old Man with a conundrum. To begin with, he insisted on being called Tim. Nowhere in Lang's records had the nickname "Tim" previously appeared. Tim told him Chief Keller had renamed him that very morning. His personnel file indicated his mother was dead and that he had also lost one of his sisters. The file did not indicate the circumstances and Tim had been evasive when questioned about their fates. Otherwise, Tim's sub school grades were exemplary. His fitness scores were flawless and he was genuinely enthusiastic about his assignment to Tunny. His apparent quick acceptance of his new nickname and the display of loyalty to Chief Keller were admirable. When asked about his experience with firearms, though, Tim said he had none. But his hesitation before answering that question led Browne to suspect otherwise. Browne put a hold on Lang's secret clearance until he could get more details from ONI (Office of Naval Intelligence) about his personal background. He made a note to Hennessey to fire off such a request and ask for an expedited return.

Roger Roads wouldn't make it. Browne was as sure of this as he was of his son's love. Roads didn't have the backbone—oh, he was smart enough—but he lacked the courage and determination to complete the rigors of submarine qualifications. His mother had married and divorced twice during Roads' childhood. He was her only son and she had made it difficult for him to enter military service. Only after it became clear that he would be drafted had she relented and agreed to his service in the Navy.

Roads had grown up around women and they had doted on him as the only male child. His Grandmother, sister, and aunts had spoiled him with affection and showered him with easy praise. Life had never presented a challenge for young Roger, his women saw to that. Bad grades at Hollywood High School resulted in a parent-teacher conference. Teachers can be easily influenced by a star of stage and screen like Natalie Roads. Aunt Mary Roads was a diva in her own right and Grandmother Florence Roads had been a silent film star. This pampered, prestigious background embarrassed Roger and he avoided discussing it with his friends and shipmates. Only the Old Man knew who his family really was.

But Bill Browne saw the weakness in Roger's demeanor and felt the softness in his handshake. No, thought Captain Browne, the boy will buckle under the pressure and be sent home to Mommy within a few months. He'd stake his gold oak leaves on it!

The Old Man completed his interviews and initialed the ship's log entries made by Hennessey. He censored the letters written by his new crewmen. David's letter was sassy and full of false bravado. A couple of weeks at sea would calm that attitude.

Tim's letter was dark and a little mysterious. He had written his sister, Alice. Tim made references to his new surroundings and a "fresh start." Bill didn't like the sound of that—he didn't want any surprises from the crew while Tunny was bottomed in hostile waters.

Simon's letter was factual and boring. He wrote exactly what was prescribed and no more. Bill felt like he was reading a phone book.

Roger's letter would require a great deal of cutting and pasting. He had almost parroted the Skipper's entire welcome speech in his missive to his Mother. Captain Browne marked out the parts that were classified and his Mother was left with a salutation and a "Lovingly Yours" closing. He called Hennessey into the wardroom and told him to have Roads perform a rewrite under the Yeoman's watchful eye. Browne was pissed off as Hennessey could tell when he got his instructions for Roads.

Browne then left the confines of the forward battery to inspect his boat. Forward battery was officers' country. The COB and two other senior CPO's shared quarters in this compartment, as well. The CPO's Forward Battery berthing space was called the "Goat Locker."

Tunny's cigar-shaped pressure hull included seven watertight compartments and two "bubble" compartments perched atop the main pressure hull. From forward aft these compartments started with the Forward Torpedo Room, in familiar jargon simply called the Forward Room. Tunny's main armament of four torpedo tubes was located in this compartment. Two of the original six tubes had been replaced by missile fire control instrumentation when the Regulus missiles were installed. These electronics were removed when Tunny was again refitted as an APSS (Attack Personnel Submersible). Lockers were installed instead and scuba diving gear was stored there now.

Officers' Country in the Forward Battery are just aft of the Forward Room. The Captain's Quarter's, the Ship's office and the rest of the boat's officer complement berthed in the Forward Battery.

In the bilge of this compartment were installed 126 wet cell DC batteries, similar to those used to start automobiles. A similar number of wet cells were located in the bilge of the After Battery Compartment. This redundancy insured that Tunny always had propulsion power available should one set of batteries be lost. Battery power was used exclusively during submerged operations. Tunny could make eight knots submerged for 30 minutes or one knot for thirty-six hours before the batteries had to be recharged.

Immediately aft of the Forward Battery was the Control Room. Control was the nerve center of Tunny. Here were located the trim manifold, the high-pressure air manifold and the hydraulic manifold. Over the hydraulic manifold was located a series of red lights. This set of lights was called the "Christmas Tree." Red lights oriented as horizontal dashes indicated a major hull opening (either a large hull valve or a watertight hatch) was shut. Under these dashed red lights were red circular lights. When these red circular lights were illuminated, the corresponding hull opening was open.

Also located in Control were the bow and stern diving planes controls. The bow planes were rigged out in the process of a dive and they controlled Tunny's depth. The stern planes were permanently rigged out and they controlled Tunny's angle of dive or surface. Depth to keel was read from the depth gauge, which was translated from water pressure. Diving angle was read on a mechanical gauge which measured angles of 10 degrees or more from horizontal. As a backup to the inclinometer gauge, a bubble device, similar to a carpenter's level, was also close at hand.

Squeezed in amidships between the air manifold and the trim manifold was the radio room. This was a comparably spacious area because more of Tunny's missile control instrumentation had been located here. Now it was continuously manned by the duty radioman. It was off limits to almost all personnel and qualifications required only a cursory knowledge of the operations in this top-secret area. The control room lower level housed the pump room where the main hydraulic accumulator and the trim and drain pumps were located. Also in the Control Room bilge, just forward of the pump room, was the sonar equipment. This area was of vital importance during bottoming and special operations.

A ladder ascended from the middle of Control into the Conning Tower above. The Conning Tower (Conn) was a bubble compartment separated from the rest of the boat by a watertight hatch. During normal operations, the watertight hatch would remain open to allow voice communications between the diving officer in Control and the conning officer on the periscope. In the Conn were located Tunny's helm, all navigation equipment, radar and compass repeaters, the dead reckoning plotter (DRT), the torpedo data computer (TDC), underwater telephone (UQC) and both periscopes. During submerged and bottoming operations, the Conn acted as the boat's bridge. Another watertight hatch led upward to the surface bridge topside.

Tunny's sail was of a configuration called a "step sail." The bridge was located just above the forward end of the Conning Tower and gave an appearance that the sail had a step in it. Here was where most surface watches were stood by the Officer of the Deck (OOD). He was assisted by lookouts stationed on the port and starboard sides of the Bridge. The very top of the sail had holes that allowed the periscopes, radar antennae, radio antennae and the snorkel induction and exhaust valves to be extended toward the surface when submerged. Each of these masts were housed within Tunny's sail when they were fully retracted.

Moving aft of Control, Browne entered the After Battery Compartment. Besides the 126 wet cell batteries located in this compartment's bilge, here was also the crews' galley and mess, a large portion of the crew's berthing and the ship's refrigerator and freezer. The Skipper exchanged some small talk with the commissaryman, the mess cook and a few others gathered around the tables in the mess area. He then continued aft past the crew's head and shower room and ducked through the watertight door into the Forward Engine Room.

Only one large diesel engine remained in Tunny's Engine's Forward Compartment. Her pony engine, a small six cylinder diesel, had also been removed from below decks to accommodate the increased air conditioning requirements of the hangar and to remove the heat generated by the missile fire-control electronics associated with the Regulus ICBM's. Engines Forward now housed a single Fairbanks-Morse nine-cylinder, 8 1/8" x 10" opposed piston diesel engine. This massive prime mover drove an electric generator that, in turn, produced 600 volts of direct current electricity on demand. The men that worked in Engines Forward and Engines Aft (the next compartment astern) were the hardest working members of

Browne's crew. In addition to the engines, HVAC plants, high-pressure air compressors and sea water distilling plants were located here.

All of this constantly moving equipment that was over 25 years from a new condition, presented these men with continual operation and maintenance problems. Browne could never remember seeing a "snipe" (a member of the "black gang") without grease on their clothes or bodies. The Chief Engineer, a twenty-five year Navy submarine veteran with a WWII combat patrol pin named Emile Gordon, was Browne's worst discipline problem. Browne tolerated him because he got the most from his men and machinery. Chief Gordon was at this moment in the Brig. He and a few of his fellow snipes had turned Pauline's (a local night spot and whorehouse) into a shambles the previous night.

It seems that they all decided that they looked better naked than did the strippers. This sound judgment was based upon the reasoning fouled by six quarts of Tanduhay Rum and about two cases of San Miguel beer for chasers.

Gordon had also performed his patented "flaming moon" dance the previous night. When drunk, Chief Gordon would drop his pants and stuff one end of a 20' section of toilet paper in his butt crack. One of his loyal snipes would light the other end on fire and Gordon would dance provocatively atop one of Pauline's tables until he felt his ass begin to warm. Then he would reach around and remove the flaming paper from his butt before it began to burn his hemorrhoids.

However, on this particular evening he had gotten so drunk that he couldn't find his ass with either hand. The flaming TP had extinguished itself between his butt cheeks. Legend had it that the smell of burned hair and hemorrhoids lingered in Paulines the rest of the night.

Finally, the Marines in Pauline's at the time, also fortified with several San Miguel's, thought they were better suited for burlesque than were the drunken sailors. This difference of opinion quickly deteriorated into a brawl. A call went out to the Shore Patrol who arrived with two paddy wagons from the Marine guard. The Shore Patrol loaded everyone, Marines, sailors, and strippers into the paddy wagons and transported them to the base Brig. That morning, the day after Christmas, Browne had been to the Brig to collect his recalcitrant black gang and their Chief Petty Officer.

It took super-human restraint for him to refrain from laughing at the sight of this pitiful crew. Various costumes comprised of strippers' boas, Marine trousers and sailors' white hats adorned the humanity collected in the cell. Chief Gordon wore nothing but his shoes and socks (someone had bandaged his ass with gauze) and was still passed out cold on the cell floor. His crew, the strippers, and the Marines were awake, but suffering the ill effects of 150 proof rum and beer chasers. Browne had his hung-over snipes released and had Gordon removed to a more comfortable cell where he instructed the Shore Patrol to send him back to Tunny when he awoke and found proper attire.

The Maneuvering Room is the electrical switch box of any submarine and directly aft of the After Engine Room. Here the Direct Current (DC) electricity generated by the diesel engine's attached generators is distributed to perform the various functions critical to the boat's mission. Some of the power is converted to Alternating Current (AC) to power pump motors, cooking equipment, distilling plants, electronic components, lighting, etc. But most of the DC power is used to drive the four massive direct current motors bolted, two each, to Tunny's two main drive shafts.

These shafts were affixed to the twin propellers (screws, in Navy parlance) that drove Tunny through the sea. Electric switch settings were made by electrician's mate watchstanders in this compartment and were vital to every operation Tunny needed to complete. Without the distribution station in Maneuvering and the DC generators in the two engine rooms, Tunny would be nothing but a cork with a rather fancy retractable telescope. Browne's experience on Chopper enhanced his respect for the crew members that manned of this vital space.

The Stern Room or the After Torpedo Room is the last compartment aft, hence its cryptic name. This compartment was used mostly for crew's berthing. All four torpedo tubes originally installed in Tunny's After Room had long since been removed and replaced with berthing and locker space. Browne walked slowly through this compartment, stooping often to peer outboard of the stowed gear. These outboard nooks and crannies were ideal places for exhausted nonquals to curl up and skylark for a few hours. He had discovered these secret places when he was qualifying on USS Grouper out of New London. That seemed a lifetime ago.

Seeing no life outboard, Browne grabbed the ladder and ascended to Tunny's fantail. Looking forward at the massive hangar affixed to Tunny's pressure hull aft of her sail, he shook his head in marvel and shame. A Gato class boat was a sleek, menacing man-o-war whose sisters wrought havoc upon the Japanese fleet during the last war. These boats, Tunny included, sunk the majority of enemy merchant shipping during that conflict. In the process, almost one-third of the crews that manned them never returned—the highest loss ratio sustained by any branch of the US military service. And here Tunny sat today, with this hideous bubble welded to her hull that made her look like a pregnant guppy that died in childbirth.

Her hangar door stood open and the deck crew was maintaining some of the equipment stowed hastily from their last mission to the Vietnamese coast. Chief Keller had his Torpedomen break down the small arms to clean and oil them for their next visit to hostile shores. The UDT preferred not to have to use these lethal tools, since their missions were all covert. A successful mission did not include the discharge of any of these weapons. So far, all Tunny's missions had been successful while under Browne's command.

The Skipper checked his watch. It was 1715 hours and Emily would be on the pier with Billy waiting for him. He and Keller exchanged greetings as he rushed forward to the gangway and his little family. Since he had taken command of this vessel, he had learned to cherish every moment with them. He found himself memorizing trivial things like the way Emily moved about the kitchen when she cooked or the way young Billy held his spoon during his first attempts to feed himself.

He had never known anyone like Emily before. They had met at a Youngster Class mixer at one of his friend's homes in Baltimore when he was at Annapolis. She hadn't caught his eye at first. She was with the most attractive blonde he had ever seen. He had begun to calculate his CPA (Closest Point of Attack) to the blonde, when another of his classmates beat him to her and took her to the dance floor. Almost as an after thought, he continued on his course toward the now vacant berth. Pulling alongside Emily, he threw over his first line in an attempt to tie up outboard.

"Hi," he said, "Wanta dance?"

"Sorry, sailor," said Emily, "I've been ordered not to lose this chair for any reason. Getting another place to sit this evening may be impossible. Why don't you sit down and wait till Missy, the tall blonde, comes back from this dance. That's why you came over here anyway, isn't it?"

"Ahhh, well, I ahhh, just thought you might, ahhh," stammered Bill. He felt his face turn red and he began to perspire.

"Oh, just sit down! Quit acting like a schoolboy caught with his hand in the cookie jar!" scolded Emily. "I've been through this routine before. Missy catches everyone's eye. It's like she has neon lights attached to her, the way guys stare."

As ordered, Bill sat. "You're right," he said, "she is stunning."

Emily laughed and they began to talk. Then they danced and talked—then they sat again and talked some more. By the time Bill dropped her off at her dormitory door early the next morning, he was infatuated. He realized now that he was just infatuated then. Today he was in love—deeply and eternally. His life without Emily and Billy was unimaginable; so he hurried to the gangway, saluted the topside watch and the colors and clambered ashore for a much-anticipated evening with his family. Soon Tunny would once more be asked to travel in harm's way—and he would have to lead her there.

Chapter Seven

Liberty

At 1600 hours, the workday on Tunny ended. The duty section, Section Three, secured the fire watches where there had been welders aboard and relieved the topside and below decks watch. They had been through this routine countless times before—it was almost automatic. The men assigned to Sections One and Two hit the showers or headed for the barracks. It was time for liberty!

"Okay, men," said Keller, "you can hit the beach. But be back aboard the base by midnight. Your liberty passes are not valid after midnight. Try to come back after then and you'll have to stand before Captain's Mast."

Captain's Mast is standard non-judicial punishment meted out by the Skipper. His prerogatives for punishment of rules violations were wide-ranging. Usually, though, Browne simply denied liberty privileges for a few days.

The midnight liberty privilege is called "Cinderella Liberty" for obvious reasons. But it was still adequate time to blow off steam, get drunk, and get laid if the liberty port was Olongapo. For a couple of kids fresh from "the world," Olongapo was the equivalent of an adult amusement park.

Lang and Roads followed Woods and Rance to the barracks with their duffle bags in tow. Few personal belongings were kept in the Crew's Barracks. When Tunny arrived in Subic in August of 1966 there was no barracks for her crew. Standard policy was that ship's crews didn't rate ashore billeting. This wasn't a problem for all the other ships which were on six month deployment to the Western Pacific. However, as the only home-ported ship in Subic, Captain

Browne had other ideas on that subject. Over a period of several months, he personally used stealth, guile and brute force to get the Naval Station command to turn over an obsolete old building for the crew's use. It wasn't much, but it was a lot better than the tight living quarters on board Tunny.

Usually some civilian clothes, some toiletries, and perhaps a radio or tape player were stowed in the barracks. The crew also had to provide their personal bedding and towels. Bunks weren't assigned because the barracks was truly a temporary quarters. Most Tunny sailors used the barracks as a place to shower and change into civvies before hitting the beach. It was also used on the return trip after Cinderella Liberty was over to change back into dungarees before reporting back aboard. In addition, the barracks provided ready access to the base laundry service—another civilian contractor cleared for base entry.

Lang and Roads had been invited by Woods and Rance to join them for liberty that evening. After the obstacle course prank, it was with some trepidation that Tim and Roger agreed to be escorted by the lead pranksters. But they were new in town and felt the need for tour guides, no matter how uncertain they were of the guides' motives.

After changing into civvies, the four sailors hailed a base cab for the mile and a half journey to the Main Gate. The cab stopped about 50 yards from the Marine guard post they had passed through less than 24 hours prior. They encountered a monument at this gate they hadn't noticed on the previous evening. It commemorated the US Navy's conquest of the Spanish Navy in 1898. The Spanish-American War had reached all the way to the Philippine Islands. Admiral Dewey had defeated a vastly outgunned and out maneuvered Spanish fleet in Manila Bay to secure the Philippines for the United States of America. The monument the Tunny sailors passed nonchalantly was the remnants of the Old Spanish Gate—the traditional entrance to the base at Subic Bay.

They displayed their liberty cards and military ID's to the Marine guards and walked across the bridge over the Santa Rita River.

"Smell that?" said Jim Woods. "This is Shit River! It only gets worse from here!" Jim and Eddie laughed in a conspiratorial way and exchanged glances with the wide-eyed newcomers.

Before them, separating the Navy Base from the tank town of

Olongapo was the Santa Rita River, affectionately called "Shit River" by the base occupants. Olongapo, like most Philippine towns, did not have an underground sewage system. Instead, the denizens discharged their sewage into a series of open ditches (locally called Benjo ditches) that, in turn, flowed into the Santa Rita. During the monsoon season, daily rainfall cleansed the "sewer system" enough to remove most offending odors. But it was now December and the monsoons were five months away; hence the pervasive smell of human waste.

Below the bridge over the Santa Rita, floating on the copper-colored water were small canoe-like vessels the locals called banca boats. The crew of these small craft were 12 to 14 year old children begging for coins from the liberty-bound sailors. Shapely young Filipina maidens danced provocatively in some of the banca boats, further enticing the sailors to part with their coinage.

Out of curiosity, more than anything, Tim dug a quarter from his jeans and tossed it toward one of the boats below. His aim was bad and the coin fell short of its intended target. Almost before the quarter hit the putrid contents of Shit River, several young divers went in after the coin. How these young swimmers could find the coin in the fouled waters at night would remain a mystery to Roger and Tim for the rest of their lives.

The liberty crew's first encounter with Olongapo's occupants was with money changers. Jim and Eddie passed several exchange booths until they came to one particularly colorful establishment with a sign in English that read, "Uncle Sam's Foreign Exchange."

"This is the best place to change your bucks into pesos," said Eddie. "Uncle Sam's a friend of ours. Tunny sailors get a special deal here. We'll vouch for you this first time, but next time wear your whites on the beach so Sam can see your ship's patch." The ship's patch was a small white-on-navy blue piece of fabric that was sewn to the top of every sailor's left sleeve. The patch bore the name of the ship to which the sailor was assigned. Apparently, Sam accepted this insignia as a Tunny sailor's bona fide. They exchanged $10.00 for 42 Philippine pesos. All Tunny sailors got an extra 2 pesos from Sam because their ship was home ported in Subic and they were frequent Olongapo visitors.

At the end of the row of moneychangers was an enormous

cabstand with about two dozen jitney cabs waiting for fares. A jitney was a jeep-like vehicle, flamboyantly decorated, that had been modified to allow easy entry and exit for passengers. They were all four-wheel drive vehicles; the rains of the monsoon season required this special feature. The capacity of jitneys varied from four to ten crowded occupants.

"Take us to the Home Port," yelled Woodsey.

"I know betta place for sailor boys," replied the jitney driver in broken English. "Give you free blow job when you buy five drinks for bar girl." The driver spoke with what seemed to be a Spanish accent. The accent was most familiar to Tim, a native Texan. It occurred to him that the vestiges of Spain's occupation had not been completely eradicated by Ugly Americans.

"No!" Eddie's reply was indignant and firm. "We said Home Port and we fuckin' mean it!" Turning to Tim and Roger, Eddie said, "These guys get some kinda commission if they bring in new business to one of the bars along Magsaysay. But you never know who's waiting for ya when you get outta the cab. One guy off Oriskany took one o' these drivers up on his bargain and never came back. Ya gotta be careful!" Now Tim and Roger knew why they had chosen to be guided on their first Olongapo liberty.

Rather than risk losing the fare, the driver nodded in the affirmative and shifted the cab into gear for the trek to Home Port Lounge. Trek was an apt description of the less than one-half mile journey to Home Port. Magsaysay Avenue was a morass of potholes and bumps that sometimes threatened to swallow or overturn the tiny cab. The monsoon rains played havoc on Olongapo's streets. Asphalt paving was often installed, but could never successfully adhere through one rainy season. When the volume of rain exceeded 10" per hour, as it often did between May and September in this latitude, nothing that was not permanently attached below ground would remain undamaged.

Only two streets in Olongapo were "On Limits" to US military personnel. Magsaysay and Rizal were the main avenues of this tank town and everything one building lot off these streets was forbidden to US military access.

Every port visited by the US Navy had such avenues. In San Diego the street was named Broadway; in Seattle it was Pine Street;

in Honolulu it was Hotel Street and so on. These notorious byways expedited the sailors on their way to their peculiar form of entertainment. Usually that involved copious volumes of liquor and easy women. The Home Port Lounge was the Tunny sailors' chosen hangout in Olongapo.

Home Port was at the intersection of Magsaysay and Rizal. It was not the flashiest saloon in town, but the proprietor had entered into a sort of special arrangement with the enlisted crew of Tunny. Because sub sailors were better paid then "surface skimmers" ($50.00 per month extra in hazardous duty pay), this arrangement proved to be quite lucrative for May Chang, the Chinese madam who owned Home Port. The sailors of Tunny were given special rates for drinks they bought for the "bar hogs" and discounted rates on the adjoining hotel/whorehouse. They paid full price, though, for the pleasures of her girls' company. In addition, if a sailor wanted to extend his Cinderella liberty beyond midnight, May Chang would hide the offender by misleading the Shore Patrol.

The short, albeit painful, journey to the specified bar was enormously entertaining to the newcomers. They passed several dozen bars, restaurants, "hotels", and street vendors along the way. Once out of the aromatic presence of Shit River, Tim and Roger became aware of the unmistakable smell of barbeque. In fact, enterprising street vendors were operating several charcoal brassieres on the sidewalks of Magsaysay Avenue. But closer inspection of the cooked fare shocked them. It appeared that small children were skewered over the coals and were being roasted.

"What the fuck are those guys cookin'?" yelled Tim.

"God damn! They're cannibals!" said Roger, with a look of horror on his face.

With this, Woodsey and Eddie broke into sidesplitting laughter. "Them's monkeys bein' cooked, you idiots!" said Jim Woods. "'Course, I guess I can't blame you for mistakin' them for babies. That's what I thought when I first saw 'em."

"Wait till you guys try a baloot! You'll love that little taste treat. The bar hogs eat 'em like candy," said Eddie Rance. The smile on his face served as a warning to the fast learning new sailors. Baloots were immediately placed on their list of questionable experiences yet to be encountered.

The cab pulled up to the walk fronting the Home Port and the four young men dismounted. They split the cab fare, about two pesos, and entered the bar. Immediately, one of May Chang's "hostesses" recognized the neophytes. Sally grabbed her best friend, Jane, by the elbow and rushed Tim and Roger before any of the other "maidens" could steal their chance. New arrivals were prime targets for May Chang's girls. The uninitiated were easily parted from their Yankee dollars and were usually more generous than their saltier companions.

Sally grabbed Tim by the right arm and rubbed her breasts against his triceps. "You new in town, sailor? I love you, no shit! Buy me a Honda?" A smile crossed Tim's face and he couldn't help but like the small female that seemed to have become a permanent attachment to his arm. Jane was just as forward toward Roger. Tim and Roger didn't have to be told that the names Sally and Jane were aliases.

Soon they were escorted to a booth where a waiter confronted them for their orders. Sally presumed to order for them all. "Four San Miguels and two champagne cocktails."

"Just a frickin' minute," said Eddie. "Four San Miguels and two glasses of water. We ain't buyin' no fuckin' drinks for no fuckin' bar hogs, yet. We just stopped in for a cool one before we go on."

"No watta," said Sally. "We get shits and then can't work. Bring us Cokes, then."

"That's better," agreed Rance.

Tim was amazed by the surroundings. There was a Wurlitzer jukebox at one end of a stage upon which a lithe, brown skinned girl provocatively danced a strip tease. The bar was enormous and stretched the length of the room. Along the wall opposite the bar were several booths, one of which they occupied. Scattered in between were 15 or 16 tables accompanied by four chairs each. The room was dimly lit and the music was invasive. Tim raised the cold beer to his lips and guzzled. He'd been drinking beer since he was fourteen and there was nothing like the taste of a frosty Lone Star in a long neck bottle.

"This stuff goes down smoother'n a goober!" he smiled wide at his friends.

They all laughed and Roger rose to go feed the jukebox. Home Port definitely catered to a country and western crowd. The songs on the box were a variety of Hank Williams, Buck Owens, Jim Reeves, et al. Roger preferred rock'n roll to this selection of shit-kickers, but eventually selected a song by Brenda Lee that had made it to the top of the rock'n roll charts, as well.

"I'm Sorry" boomed from the Wurlitzer and almost everyone rose to dance with the closest hostess. Sally led Tim to the dance floor and Jane accosted Roger before he could return to the booth. They danced to the mournful lyrics and recalled memories of people far away and homes left behind less than a week ago. It seemed like an eternity since Roger had boarded that flight from L.A. to San Francisco.

His mother drove him to the terminal and had accompanied him to the gate. He had been home on leave for a little over four weeks from Basic Submarine School. They had argued intermittently about Roger's choice to join the Silent Service. Natalie Roads was alarmed when Roger announced his decision to go to sub school. She had pulled some strings and cashed in some favors with some studio executives just to get him in the Navy. He had refused to go to college at USC where she had arranged a scholarship. And then he had received his draft notice because of his 1A status with the county draft board. She sure as hell didn't want him in the Marines or the Army where he could end up in a foxhole in South Vietnam. But she accepted his decision to volunteer for sub duty when she was informed that all submarines were home ported in the States. It would be extremely unlikely that Roger would ever see Vietnam while in the sub service.

Her assumptions were thrown for a loop when he received orders to the Tunny in the Philippine Islands. It was certain that Tunny was home ported in The Philippines to support the US military operations in Vietnam. She immediately got on the phone to her Congressman. She arranged a rendezvous at the Beverly Hills Hilton. She'd screw the legislator blind before she would let her son head for Vietnam. In the end, he had no influence over Navy personnel assignments and she had shared her favors for naught.

She took her bitterness out on Roger for his stupidity for not going to USC in the first place. None of this would have been necessary had he just done as he was instructed and taken the scholarship. Natalie was used to getting her way. As one of the highest paid and most popular movie stars in Hollywood, her whims were rarely questioned. Roger's defiance would not be easily forgiven. She nagged him for his stubbornness and scolded him for his stupidity. By the time his leave from sub school was ending, Roger was anxious to return to his Navy duties.

Roger's grandmother, Florence, had been his safe haven. When the scenes with his Mother had gotten too intense, he would escape to his grandmother's home in Laguna Beach. They would talk and he would confide in her about his mother's tirades. Florence gave the boy much-needed displays of love and allowed him the freedom to express his feelings. Florence recognized a lack of self-confidence in Roger. His personality was the result of an over indulgent mother who deliberately discouraged the development of any kind of independence. More often than not, Roger found following his mother's ruling influence to be the easiest path. Rather than resist, he went along. Soon he began following the path of least resistance in all his interpersonal encounters.

That was until he met Sarah Rubens. Sarah's father was a studio executive at MGM and his fellow classmate at Hollywood High. Sarah was blond, beautiful, independent, and Jewish. The final trait was abhorrent to Natalie Roads. So Roger and Sarah had kept their high school romance a secret from Natalie until graduation. Then Sarah accepted a scholarship to Mary Washington College in Fredericksburg, Virginia. Mary Washington was an all-girl liberal arts college that had an excellent reputation on the East Coast for teacher education. Sarah wanted to teach and Roger wanted her to have her dream. So he applied to Georgetown University in Washington, DC to be close to Sarah.

Natalie had no intention of letting Roger that far from her sphere of influence. She arranged the USC scholarship and presented it to him only a few hours before his graduation. Along with the scholarship came an ultimatum—stop seeing that Jewish tart, Sarah Rubens, and get your act together here in LA.

The film industry is a small community nestled in a large city. Nothing and no one kept secrets for long. Natalie had tolerated Roger's Hebrew girlfriend only to cultivate her father at MGM. She wanted a screen test for a feature film due out the next year. She let Roger date Sarah and used the "childish" romance to get her foot in the door for the test. Rubens, in the end, had given the part to Jane

Fonda. Natalie Roads discovered the "betrayal" shortly before Roger's graduation. She vowed to end the romance so she stood in the way of every one of Roger's attempts to woo Sarah.

The draft notice was Roger's ticket to freedom. He only agreed to join the Navy to end his Mother's constant nagging. Once away from his Mother's controlling grip, he intended to find Sarah and resume their affair. He had begun to correspond with her from boot camp. At first, she was excited about their renewed relationship, but as the months progressed her letters became fewer and more aloof. Roger got worried that he was losing her and he saw sub school in New London, Connecticut as an opportunity to get to the East Coast and to Sarah.

The first chance he got he bought a train ticket to Fredericksburg to surprise Sarah at Mary Washington College. It only took a few hours to travel by rail to Virginia. He changed trains at Grand Central in New York and at Union Station in DC and arrived in the sleepy Southern town about noon on Saturday. He took a cab to her dormitory—the address of his many letters from boot camp. He was dressed in his dress blues and his shoes were spit shined to perfection. If one learned nothing else from the Navy, it was how to shine shoes. He waited in the shade of a large Magnolia tree in front of her dorm with a dozen roses under his arm.

He saw her first. She was walking with a tall dark haired fellow and they were holding hands. The dark haired male student leaned over and kissed Sarah on the cheek when they reached her dorm steps. She reached up, clutched his neck and kissed him fervently.

Roger dropped the roses in a campus trashcan as he headed for the train station. He didn't try to correspond with Sarah again. He got a couple of letters from her that he returned unopened while in New London. Soon even these meager attempts to stay in touch ceased to arrive. Apparently, his Mother's anti-semitisim was right.

Roger danced a few dances with the bar hog, Jane, and swilled the local beer until his head began to swim. Jane suggested they go next door and get a room in the hotel. He asked the price, but only as a stall. He turned over the remaining pesos to Jane and was led through the door to the adjoining whorehouse. Jane paid the bar bill and rented sheets from the hotel clerk.

Woodsey watched Roger leave with Jane and stopped them

before they could climb the stairs to their rented room in the whore-house. "Give me your wallet, Roger," said Woodsey. He extended his hand for the billfold.

"Why? You think I'm nuts enough to give you my wallet?" stammered Roger. His speech was thick from the affects of the beer.

"No, but you're drunk enough to let some bar hog roll you," said Woodsey.

"Just hand it over, Roger," said Tim. "Nobody's trying to fuck you over except that whore you're headin' off with."

Roger surrendered his billfold and followed an obviously disappointed Jane up the stairs to a room.

"What about you, Tim," inquired Woods. "Aren't you goin' to get your ashes hauled?"

"Nah, I think I'll just drink until I'm numb," laughed Tim.

They rejoined Eddie who was talking to a street vendor that had ventured into the lounge to peddle his wares. "Three pesos and that's it!' said Eddie.

"What the fuck are you buying?" said Tim.

"Baloots! Watch this," said Eddie to Tim and Woodsey. "Okay, ladies, dig in!"

Eddie laid the three duck eggs he had purchased from the street vendor on the table. Sally and a couple her fellow hostesses took the eggs and cracked them open on the edge of the table. Almost immediately, the sulphur dioxide smell of rotten eggs filled the bar. Tim felt the contents of his stomach begin to rise. The three bar hogs put the broken eggs to their lips and sucked the contents into their mouths. The nearly gestated duckling emerged from its shell, beak, webbed feet, feathers and all, to be completely devoured by the ladies of the evening.

Tim barely made it to the unisex restroom before his stomach regurgitated its contents. That's when his head began to throb and he felt his knees weaken. Woodsey, who had followed him to the head, caught him before he collapsed onto the piss and puke that flooded the floor of the john.

Chapter Eight

Underway

"Now hear this! Now hear this! All hands! Station the Maneuvering Watch! Station the Maneuvering Watch!" Chief Vincent shouted into the 1MC.

The Captain was on the Bridge and had the Conn. They were going to sea. The orders had come down from SubFlot Seven in Yokosuka the previous evening.

"Prepare to take on extra personnel and make all preparations for getting underway. Classified orders will arrive via courier at 0800 hours on 03 Jan 1967," had read the encrypted message.

Tunny had taken on stores and fuel overnight. She was standing by to answer bells from Engines Aft. All shore services were terminated.

Captain Browne shouted to the line handlers, "Single up all lines!" The order was repeated several times by various officers, Chiefs and the bridge phone talker who was connected to the fore and aft line handlers. The double loop was taken out of all four mooring lines and the slack was coiled on deck. The next command from the bridge was "Heave around on number 1 line, slack 4, cast off number 3."

"Port back one third. Starboard ahead one third. Left full rudder." Browne was now speaking into the 7MC—the maneuvering circuit that allowed communications from the Bridge to the Conn. The helmsman could clearly hear his voice through the open conning tower hatch.

"Port back one third. Starboard ahead one third. Left full rudder, aye sir," repeated the helmsman in the Conning Tower. LT Turner watched the helmsman ring up the ordered revolutions on the engine order telegraph. Maneuvering answered back by matching their pointers to those ordered from the Conn. "Port is answering back one third and starboard ahead one third, Sir."

The helmsman shouted, "The rudder is left full, sir!"

"Very well," acknowledged Browne. "Cast off line 4!" Followed almost immediately by, "Take in number 1." The officers and chiefs in charge of line handling repeated these orders. The line handlers on the pier removed the loop from the bollards on the pier and tossed the mooring lines to the Tunny crew. A good crew never let their mooring lines get wet and Tunny had a good crew.

Tunny's fantail began to slide away from the pier. "Starboard stop," ordered the Skipper.

He waited for the obligatory acknowledgement from the Conn, "Starboard answers stop, Sir."

"Very well. Rudder amidships," came his command.

"Rudder amidships, aye sir!" said the helmsman. Within a few seconds, Browne heard, "Rudder is amidships, sir!"

"Very well," came Browne's standard response. "All back one third." Tunny's stern had now attained enough clearance to back safely into the harbor. Tunny slid gracefully backward into Subic Bay.

"Right full rudder. All ahead two-thirds!" commanded the Skipper. He was bringing her about to head to sea. When he got her bow pointed toward the mouth of the harbor, Browne shouted, "Make your course 278, all ahead standard!"

Tunny slowly stopped moving backward and began her journey toward open water and the South China Sea. Bill stole a brief glance at the pier. Emily was holding Bill, Jr. and waving his small hand toward his Daddy in goodbye. He had lost count as to the number of times he had waved goodbye to Emily as his boat disappeared from safe harbor and went over the horizon; but he knew exactly how many times he had waved goodbye to young Billy. This was the twelfth time in his short 18-month life that young Billy had watched his Daddy go to sea. The excitement of putting to sea had long worn off and was now replaced by a sense of duty. It had become a routine much like the Manhattan executive who got on the train every morning to go to work. No, thought Bill, that was an incorrect comparison. The New York office worker had better odds for a safe return.

Below on the main deck, the line handlers, including Tim, David, Simon, and Roger, were stowing the mooring lines in line lockers. These free-flooding lockers were then secured with ratchet wrenches. The topside sound powered phone, the watch box, and the other gear were passed down to the Forward Room for stowage in their lockers. The gangway had been stowed in the superstructure as soon as the lines were singled up. LT O'Rourke made certain, as part of his duties as 1st Lieutenant, that all was in readiness for sea topside before he climbed to the bridge to report to the Old Man.

"Topside's all secure, Sir," said Mike, "and rigged for dive."

"Very well, Mike," said the Old Man. "We'll secure the Maneuvering watch as soon as we clear the last harbor buoy."

"Aye, aye, sir," replied Mike. He proceeded below to his maneuvering watch station in the Forward Room. He passed Chief Vincent at the hydraulic manifold. The COB could have chosen any station he wanted during this cycle, but Mike knew he preferred the hydraulic manifold where he could monitor all critical hull openings on the Christmas tree.

In the Conn, LT Harvey Turner was viewing Tunny's progress from the harbor through the periscope. As Tunny's navigator, he was responsible for her course. He would pass his course recommendations to the Skipper who in turn would send them on to the helmsman. The helmsman could not make take any course or rudder orders from anyone but the Officer in Charge on the bridge. During maneuvering watches, that was always the Captain.

"Recommend course 240 degrees, sir," said Turner. The course was stated one number at a time to avoid confusion. So Browne heard the course as "two four zero degrees."

"Very well. Helmsman, come right to 240 degrees," said Bill Browne.

"Coming right to 240 degrees, aye sir," said the helmsman. The helm was turned clockwise and Tunny responded by changing her heading to port.

On the helm was the senior Quartermaster, QM1 (SS) Earl "Snuffy" Smith. Snuffy was not the most experienced helmsman in Tunny, but he knew how she handled better than anyone. During a war patrol in 1944, Tunny had taken a bomb close aboard her port bow. Somehow, the explosion have bent her keel about one degree to starboard. For Tunny to steer a straight course, Snuffy had to hold her rudder one degree to port to compensate.

When the compass heading approached 235 degrees, Snuffy rotated the helm clockwise. Expertly, the compass indicator settled at 240 degrees without error. "That's perfect, old girl," thought Snuffy.

"Steady on 240 degrees, sir," shouted Snuffy.

The rudder indicator displayed one-degree port and Tunny left a perfectly straight trail of white water in her wake.

"Very well. All ahead full," commanded the Skipper.

Snuffy made the speed adjustments on the repeater in the Conn. Maneuvering answered and the entire crew could feel the increase in vibrations as the giant screws rotated faster and Tunny's speed increased.

"Answers all ahead full, sir," said Snuffy. He thought, "Hold steady, you old bucket." Snuffy loved Tunny. He had served as her Quartermaster since her days as a Regulus missile boat. Through her helm, he understood how she felt; whether she was in a good mood or a foul one. She was ready today; her time in port had given her a rest and she was anxious to get back where she belonged—at sea. Snuffy knew Tunny hated it in port, tied to a pier. She wanted the freedom of the open ocean where she relished the constant conflict with the forces of Neptune to try to sink her. She had always emerged victorious and proud, no matter what the Sea God had thrown her way. That's why Snuffy was her most ardent suitor and her most faithful comrade-in-arms against the evil forces of a hostile enemy.

Ashore, Snuffy was like Tunny—a reluctant visitor. He belonged at sea, too. He wasn't comfortable without a moving deck under his feet. It took him longer than any of Tunny's crew to lose his sea legs when on the beach. He had always been the first to find them when back at sea.

To assist him in his efforts to recover his land legs, Snuffy drank. He drank not just to quench his thirst, but he drank to become more comfortable with the land beneath his boondockers. At least, that is what he told himself.

Recently, however, Snuffy was usually ill for the first few days at sea. He experienced cold sweats accompanied by "the shakes" and he was nauseous to the point of diarrhea and vomiting. He even began to hallucinate sometimes. But the last few times out, he had drawn off about a quart of the denatured alcohol the Electronic Technicians (ET's) were issued to clean electric switches.

Snuffy then mixed the pirated alcohol with the kool-aide powder the cooks mixed with water to serve at mess. The kool-aide powder made a vile mixture the crew referred to as "bug juice." Since the powder was not a controlled substance aboard ship, Snuffy could easily obtain it from his friendly commissaryman.

Snuffy's alcohol concoction was called "gilly" and was quite common among those afflicted with alcoholism in the Navy. Alcoholic sailors on extended sea duty could forestall the tell-tale withdrawal symptoms with gilly and, thereby, continue to function at their watch stations. Were they caught intoxicated on watch, however, Captain's Mast punishments were quite severe.

In Snuffy's case, the gilly calmed his nerves, except for an almost continuous bout with of diarrhea. To counteract the effects of his affliction, Snuffy further mixed the gilly in a Kaopectate cocktail. This further disguised the drink from LT Turner, Snuffy's boss.

Like most alcoholics, Snuffy rationalized his addiction. He had convinced himself he was more of a man because he could consume gilly. No one else in Tunny would dare to drink his unusual cocktail, which made him special in his twisted estimation. After all, only true sub sailors could down gilly on a regular basis.

Unbeknownst to Snuffy, as part of a daily routine, the contents of the denatured alcohol tank in the Forward Room was carefully monitored and gauged. Every ounce had to be accounted for at the end of each watch. When Chief Keller began receiving reports of mysterious reductions in tank levels, he realized from experience that someone was drawing off the substance for their personal use.

Snuffy had been careful to tap the tank when in port and hide a small quantity in his locker. The Forward Torpedo Room was not under constant watch when Tunny was in port and this allowed him access to the tank without discovery—he thought.

Keller had assigned a special gilly watch in the Forward Room and by the process of elimination had caught Snuffy tapping the tank. He had intended to confront Snuffy over the holidays, but Snuffy had taken leave and the opportunity had never presented itself for resolution.

Now underway, Keller had been forced to confide in LT

O'Rourke about Snuffy's habit. Mike, in turn, consulted with Harvey Turner. LT Turner now had a problem he had no experience in addressing. He needed Smith's expertise in the Conn and on the helm, but he was also aware of the impact on Smith's judgment when he was intoxicated. He had seen Smith's personality undergo a transformation when he drank heavily. Snuffy became belligerent and combative. Although Smith was only about 5'5" tall, he thought he grew to over 6' when drunk and he lost all inhibitions. He started fights, strolled naked down Rizal Avenue, arrived late for quarters, and had been put on report twice in the last year for insubordination. Smith had been forced to appear at Captain's Mast to answer for his conduct.

Both times that Smith had appeared at Mast he seemed very remorseful and apologetic. He accepted his restricted liberty privileges without argument and agreed to pay the damages he had caused during his drunken rampages. But secretly, Snuffy bore a deep resentment toward Turner. He thought of Turner as a lightweight and scoffed at his limited navigational skills. When he was on liberty, he belittled Harvey to the rest of the crew. Because Snuffy was a respected Tunny veteran and his signature was required on qualifications cards, the new crewmen were forced to endure Snuffy's tirades about Harvey Turner.

Turner found himself in uncharted territory now. He was aware of Smith's resentment and his drunken dialogues with other crewmembers. But he could not draw upon any training or experience as to how to deal with the disease that was consuming a member of his department. He didn't want to tell the Skipper for fear he would lose Smith's expertise at the chart table and his skill on the helm. On the other hand, Smith's continued belligerence and defiance was detrimental to shipboard discipline and morale.

But this particular morning, Smith seemed in control of his personal demons. He was respectful and cooperative as he efficiently handled his assigned duties. He even seemed jovial as he drank Kaopectate from a coffee cup. He moved about the Conning Tower with the grace and agility that was the result of long practice. The charts of Subic Bay and the channel leading to open water were laid out on the DRT and the LORAN navigational receivers were tuned to the precise radio frequencies. Turner monitored Tunny's progress through the #1 periscope. Harvey confirmed the passage of the last harbor buoy from his station and spoke over the sound powered phone to the bridge operator, "Upon clearing the sea buoy, recommend coming to course 270."

"Aye, aye, sir," was the reply through the phone.

Captain Browne watched as Tunny cleared the sea buoy. Within seconds his voice was heard from the bridge, "Make your course 270 degrees. Secure the maneuvering watch. Set the sea watch. Rig ship for dive."

Regular watch personnel assumed their stations throughout Tunny and preparations were made to submerge Tunny once she reached the 100-fathom curve. The 100-fathom curve is a standard fathometer reading of 600 feet depth to keel. Most submarines would not perform their first dive or "trim dive" until the bottom was at this depth. In reality, Tunny often submerged in much shallower waters. Her hull had been specially prepared for shallow water operations to include bottoming.

Captain Browne called the Conning Tower for a fathometer reading. Harvey glanced at the repeater installed near the DRT and transmitted the depth reading of 350 feet to the Bridge. He also heard from the control room that Tunny had completed the preparations for diving. He informed Captain Browne, "Ship is rigged for dive, sir."

"Very well, Lieutenant." Browne replied. "Clear the Bridge! Dive! Dive!" Simultaneously, sailors assigned as lookouts scrambled from the bridge down through the Conning Tower to assume bow and stern plane stations in the Control Room below as the klaxon sounded the diving alarm.

"Aaaaooooougah!...Aaaaooooougah!"

The twice-repeated sounding of the klaxon sent an adrenalin rush through every member of Tunny's crew. Diesel engines ground to a halt, switches were thrown in the Maneuvering Room, and hydraulically operated hull openings, including the main induction valve, were slammed shut. Chief Vincent watched the lights on the Christmas tree as they all changed from circles to dashes. When they were all indicating dashes, he shouted, "Straight board!"

O'Rourke had appeared from the Forward Room to assume duties as diving officer for this duty section. Mike shouted to the stern planesman, "Five degrees down angle on the stern planes!" And to the bow planesman, "Make your depth five-five feet!"

When the depth gauge read 35 feet, O'Rourke gave the command, "Blow negative to the mark!" Petty Officer 2nd Class Edward Rance opened the high-pressure air valve for negative tank that forced the water from the tank to sea. Theoretically, if Tunny were in perfect trim with respect to the water conditions, the evacuation of negative tank down to "the mark" would make Tunny assume neutral buoyancy. Neutral buoyancy meant that both the centers of gravity and buoyancy were in balance, allowing Tunny to easily maintain her assigned depth. This almost never happened on any submarine's first dive after an extended port visit. Increased fuel stocks, new rations, altered weapon deployments, etc. increased and shifted the displacement and balance of Tunny while she was tied to the pier. Hence, the trim dives at the 100-fathom curve. This dive allowed Tunny to reconfigure the ballast in her trim tanks to compensate for these new loading conditions.

David, Tim, and Simon watched with fascination from their assigned apprenticeship posts as Tunny's crew went through the routine they were trained to accomplish. They worked as a well-oiled machine in which all parts completed their functions precisely. There were no wasted motions, no unsure actions, and no hesitations. Every movement had been rehearsed literally hundreds of times and the sequence of events was indelible. Nothing was done without an order and every order was completed without question.

Roger began to feel suffocated. There seemed to be a great weight on his chest and his breathing became short and shallow. He had experienced this sensation before in sub school; both during ascent training and pressure tank testing. As he had done then, he managed to overcome the onset of panic through sheer will of mind. He thought of other things beyond his current situation, thus becoming almost oblivious to his surroundings and the actions of his shipmates. He never heard O'Rourke as he began to trim the ship.

"One degree up angle on the stern planes!" was O'Rourke's order as Tunny approached 55'. "Steady on 55 feet!"

The planesmen repeated the orders and confirmed their execution. Mike began trimming the boat by flooding, pumping, and shifting seawater among Tunny's various trim tanks. The Captain ordered Tunny to proceed at a dead slow speed to maintain way on the boat and still allow O'Rourke to trim the ship.

It took Mike and Woodsy, the trim manifold operator, about 15 minutes to bring Tunny back to a balanced trim. In the meantime, the Skipper maintained contact with the surface world through the periscope. A radio mast was also raised to allow LORAN reception.

Once this routine cycle was complete, Tunny was ordered to surface and proceed on a westerly course toward the Gulf of Tonkin and Southeast Asian waters. Harvey Turner, as Navigator, provided a recommended course to the Bridge and this heading was ordered. Tunny proceeded on the surface at full speed toward the Vietnamese Conflict.

Chapter Nine

Tigers

Bill Browne had realized when he took command of Tunny that his crew lacked some specialized training. Since Boatswains Mates and Gunners Mates are not part of a regulation submarine crew, no one assigned to Tunny had the unique training these Navy rates possessed. Captain Browne would have to improvise and adapt.

One day in March, Bill made a call on the Marine guard barracks at Subic Bay Naval Station. He was familiar with many of the Marines assigned to guard the largest US Navy base in the world. His routine duties and travel about the base had brought him in contact with many of the young jarheads in the guard battalion. But today he was on a special mission.

Bill entered the guard barracks and proceeded to the office of the Officer in Charge. Lieutenant Colonel Edward J. Mason was from East Saint Louis, Missouri. He had grown to manhood in the segregated slums of that city and he was as hard-bitten as that gang culture could make a man and still let him survive.

Mason had joined the Corps on a dare from his parish priest. The priest was a wily cleric that saw a chance to save one special soul from a life of trouble. Mason eventually grew to love the Corps and was determined to make a career in its service. He took advantage of the opportunity to attend college on a military scholarship and earned his gold Second Lieutenants bars upon graduation. He was assigned to a rifle platoon and quickly earned a promotion to the rank of Captain. During his first tour in Vietnam, he was awarded the Silver Star for valor and was subsequently promoted to Major.

It was during his second Vietnam tour that he was severely

wounded. He had just been promoted to Lieutenant Colonel when his battalion came under attack at Play Ku. Ed Mason was hit by shrapnel and lost the use of his left eye. After several months of rehabilitation, he was assigned to command the Marine guard at Subic.

In many ways he felt fortunate. He wasn't forced to resign from his beloved Corps, but he realized that his wound would keep him from combat action for the rest of his career. While he recognized his good fortune, he resented being relegated to a back-water service station and being put on guard duty. He longed for the excitement and authority of commanding men in combat.

He was writing his third "Request for Transfer" when Bill Browne entered his office that sultry spring day.

"CDR Browne," he greeted Bill formally. "Please have a seat. I'll just be a few minutes here." Bill Browne had received his promotion to Commander in February.

Bill Browne bristled at being delayed by the completion of some kind of bureaucratic paperwork. He settled into one of the wooden chairs in front of Mason's desk, pulling it to the polished desk top. Bill placed his cover on the desk and folded his arms across his chest. His back was ramrod straight and his feet were flat on the floor. He was here on serious business and he wanted Mason to get his message through his very formal conduct and reserved presence.

Mason couldn't help but get a message that this ships' captain was here on a mission. He glanced into Browne's eyes and discerned from Bill's expression that his transfer request could wait a few minutes. He placed his pen on the desk and slid the papers aside.

"What can I do for you Commander Browne?"

Bill leaned forward and rested his arms on Mason's desk. "I need your help." His voice was deadpan and his stare penetrated Mason's skull.

"Your men have a special training that some of my crew require. Our mission often puts us ashore in Vietnam or in other hostile areas." Bill had lowered his voice and the conspiratorial inflection was too obvious for Mason to miss.

"I am looking for a few of your Marines to provide some of my crew with small arms and squad tactics training. They will need to go through an expedited Marine boot camp. I can only spare them for about a month, but I want them to be able to protect themselves and their shipmates in the event they come in contact with a hostile force. Do you get my drift, Colonel Mason, sir?" Bill had not minced words. He did not have the luxury of time. The niceties of military protocol, Mason was an equal rank but had seniority, would only delay the safety of his crew and the accomplishment of Tunny's mission.

Mason could sense the urgency in Browne's message. "Commander Browne, what can my Marines and I do to help you? Do you want us to conduct the boot camp you are requesting?"

"That is the nature of this call, Colonel. I need experienced people to train my men. I don't have time to go through regular channels and my crew can't be spared from their official duties to attend a full-blown training school. As you might already have suspected, this training will be unofficial and top secret—even from top Navy brass. Can you help?"

Mason was intrigued. In fact, he was inspired. This was a way for him to get back in action, even if it was only vicariously through a bunch of Navy pukes.

"Commander Browne, give me three days. Bring your men to the Marine guard barracks on Monday. All they will need is their dungarees and a toothbrush. Let me have them for four weeks and I'll make them into boot Marines. Can you do that?"

Bill reached his right hand across Mason's desk. Mason grabbed it and they shook vigorously. A conspiracy had just been born—the two military officers smiled with the knowledge that their plan could never be officially reported. The machinations of the Defense Department bureaucracy would never sanction this scheme. It was too logical—it made too much common sense. Nonetheless, each man—Browne and Mason—knew they were acting in the best interests of those under their command and in the best interests of the country they proudly served. Besides, this could be fun.

Roger, Tim, Simon, and David were in the group who marched with military precision to the Marine barracks that next Monday. In all, eight of Chief Keller's torpedo crew were assigned to train as Bill

Browne's Tunny Tigers. Mike O'Rourke led the formation and counted cadence as they proceeded toward their four weeks of intensive jungle training.

The four week "school", as it was entered in Tunny's logbook, placed some of the regular sea watch back on a port and starboard routine. Bill realized that this short-handed deployment would put a strain on the rest of the crew. He could only hope they understood the necessity of their sacrifice. Only Snuffy Smith complained.

The second the Tunny sailors entered the Marine barracks the training commenced. Marine boot camp is designed to remove any sense of individuality from the recruits. As Mason had designed the course, the Tigers were immediately confronted with mental and physical stress.

They were issued identical uniforms shortly after they visited the barber. In their new apparel and with their tonsorial reformation, it became very difficult to distinguish one from another. The change in appearance further removed any sense of individuality. Mason wanted these swabbies to be a team—not a gathering of personalities.

For the next four weeks, the Tigers were subjected to a training regimen that the Marine Corps was infamous in conducting. Because the time was short for their training, Mason kept them at it for long hours—reveille was at sunrise and taps was sounded well after midnight.

Night training was the most intense. Browne and Mason conspired to develop a training schedule that emphasized nighttime operations. The nature of Tunny's clandestine missions required the cover of night.

Roger was exhausted after the first two weeks. The Marines had really worked them over on this particular day. They had hiked twenty miles around the base with 80 pounds of rocks on their backs. The shoulder harness of the backpack had bruised Roger's flesh. He never complained until he tripped over a tree root and fell awkwardly on his face. The Marine Gunnery Sergeant whacked him on the head.

"Git up, you little pussy! You gotta learn to put one boondocker in front of another without fallin' on your fuckin' face. Now git up and git movin'! The whole damn team is countin' on you, numb nuts!" The Gunny was ruthless.

The sailors from Tunny were covered in perspiration. They didn't have a dry stitch on their bodies. But the Gunny was as cool as ice—even if the temperature was over 90 degrees in the shade. His starched GI dungarees didn't reveal a drop of sweat and he looked like he had just dressed for guard duty.

That night, Tim and Roger shared a hastily constructed shelter of sticks and palm fronds. It was well after 0200 when they crawled into their makeshift beds. Tim heard Roger snoring even before his head hit the ground.

About 0330, Tim awoke to something moving next to him. He was groggy from sleep deprivation and he wasn't sure what awoke him. He reached out his hand to see what was making the noise.

He felt something with a smooth, scaly surface and it cool to the touch. He froze! Slowly he withdrew his hand. He heard a hissing sound come from the shadows of the jungle shelter.

Tim was wide awake now. Roger slept on—snoring rhythmically. Tim deliberately and slowly began to crawl from the shelter. He took care not to make any sudden movements. The hissing sound was now closer. Tim turned his head to stare directly into the red, glowing eyes of a two foot long monitor lizard. The lizard rested squarely on Roger's chest, rising and falling with the movement of Roger's diaphragm.

Tim slid his hand around Roger's foot and slowly squeezed. The snoring stopped.

"Roger," whispered Tim, "don't move."

"Huh?" Roger was still not fully awake.

"Don't move!" repeated Tim a little louder.

"God damn it, Tim, leggo my foot! That hurts, you sonofabitch!" Roger shouted.

The lizard dug his claws into Roger's stomach just before jumping to the wall of the shelter. The lizard latched on to the palm fronds and hissed a warning as he lashed the air with his green tongue.

Tim rolled free of the shelter. Roger belatedly understood the nature of his predicament. He stood straight up through the roof of the hastily constructed lean-to. The lizard was thrown into the air, hissing loudly as it hurtled end-over-end toward the Gunny's pup tent.

Roger, standing in the middle of the remains of his and Tim's handmade domicile, tried to run in the opposite direction. His feet became tangled in the construction material causing him to fall awkwardly.

The lizard flew through the Gunny's pup tent opening and landed with a thud between the supine sergeant's legs. It then beat a hasty exit over the Gunny's startled body and disappeared into the Philippine jungle.

The outburst from the Gunnery Sergeant became a thing of legend. Even Tunny sailors blushed at the vulgarity the Gunny used that evening. Most of the Marine's tirade was directed at Roger and Tim. However, it became clear that he was merely venting his fright after being awakened by a flying dragon.

Tears of laughter streamed from Tim's tired eyes as both Roger and the Gunny scrambled to extricate themselves from the reptile and their make-shift shelters. The Gunny and Roger eventually saw the humor in their predicament and joined Tim laughing. Their communal laughter infected the rest of the camp and the story of an aerial monster became part of Tunny lore.

At the end of the four week endurance course, Tim and Roger bought the Sergeant a drunk at the Home Port.

Chapter Ten

Rendezvous

Some months later the Tunny found herself on patrol again. At 0115 local time, Tunny pulled along side the USS Iwo Jima. Iwo was a specially constructed amphibious carrier equipped to handle helicopters and Harrier jump jet aircraft. She now carried a battalion of battle ready Marines and the aircraft needed to take them ashore.

But Tunny wasn't here to take on Marines. Underwater Demolition Team (UDT) 12 was standing by at the Jacob's ladder with all their gear. Tunny maneuvered close aboard and threw over two single lines that held her steady to Iwo's starboard side. Nonetheless, the weather deck of Iwo was a full 90 feet above Tunny's teakwood planked main deck.

Tunny raised her hangar door and received the UDT gear on her after deck. A cargo net and a gantry crane lowered the materials as directed by Chief Keller. The deck crew stowed the gear in the hangar and lashed it to the hangar deck. The eight-man UDT unit descended the Jacob's ladder and were greeted by Captain Browne. They saluted formally and handed Tunny their orders. Browne had Chief Vincent escort the frogmen through the Forward Room escape trunk to the wardroom.

Browne climbed to the bridge and checked to see that all personnel and equipment were aboard and properly stowed. Browne ordered Tunny to cast off from Iwo. By 0200, Tunny was at periscope depth in the Gulf of Tonkin and heading toward the coast of North Vietnam.

It was tight quarters in the wardroom; seven of Tunny's eight officers, the COB and LT Ralph Anderson of Team 12 managed to squeeze in. They had before them on the wardroom table a chart of the harbor entrance into Haiphong, North Vietnam.

LT Anderson was the first to speak, "Gentlemen, we are assigned to penetrate the harbor defenses at Haiphong, map the port installations, main channels and bottom conditions and then egress without ever revealing our presence."

The officers of Tunny were speechless! Haiphong was the most heavily defended harbor in the world. The North Vietnamese had built and perfected its defenses for over 13 years, since the fall of French Indochina to the Viet Minh in 1954. The anti-ship mine fields and submarine defenses were thought to be impenetrable.

The Skipper's face began to spread into a sly grin. "This is the first time in my life in Tunny that I have ever heard this crew silent! What's the bitch, men?"

Turner, as Navigator, spoke first. "How are we supposed to get past the submarine nets and anti-ship mines, let alone navigate past high-powered shore batteries? Sir, our charts of Haiphong are from the French, who haven't been in there since the 1950's! Frankly, I wouldn't trust those charts even if the Frogs had given 'em to us when we were alongside Iwo!"

"Sir," It was O'Rourke, "Even if we go in submerged, there is little maneuvering room in those shallow waters. If we run aground, we're dead meat! All we have to defend ourselves are four fifty caliber machine guns and some M16 rifles. We might as well just use harsh language!"

LT Gary Barker, the XO, spoke next. "I'm sure the Navy has better and more current reconnaissance than the old French charts. Furthermore, the Captain wouldn't lead the boat into trouble without some kind of an out, would you sir?" the XO spoke hopefully.

"Well," said Browne. The entire wardroom of Tunny inhaled at once. If there had been an engine running on snorkel, the vacuum alarm, set at 6" of mercury, would have tripped the diesels off line. "Gentlemen, the orders are not specific about getting in and out. We are ordered to use our best judgment to accomplish the assigned mission. However, LT Anderson has some useful information that could expedite our job. LT Anderson, please!"

"Thank you, sir," said Anderson. "Gentlemen, here's the deal! Ships of neutral registry enter and leave Haiphong constantly. In two days, a certain ship of Norwegian registry will appear at the mouth of the Red River and signal for permission to enter. It is proposed that we follow that freighter into Haiphong close astern. The river is very polluted and muddy. In theory, our silhouette should not be detectable from the surface. Also, we have brought with us an audio-tape of the freighter's sound signature. This tape has been provided to your sonar room. As you are all aware, this sound signature is the equivalent to the freighter's fingerprint. No two ships in the world emit the same sounds from their screws. Your sonar operators will use this unique sound to follow the freighter through the harbor defenses into the port facilities. We are to follow the same freighter out after she completes off-loading.

"So, fellows, what do you think?" inquired Anderson.

Everyone but the XO burst into laughter. Barker was incredulous and indignant. "Who dreamt up this pea-brained scheme up anyway? The Army? To begin with, who's on this mysterious Norwegian freighter and what's to keep them from informing on us? Second, even if they Vietnamese can't see us, their sonar will pick us up before we even get to the harbor defenses!"

Gary Barker's voice had gotten louder with each spoken syllable. It had also become higher pitched. By the time he was finished, Barker was screaming at the top of his lungs. The thin curtain that served as a wardroom door could not contain the volume and intensity of his voice.

This wasn't the first time the crew had heard the XO blow his top. This characteristic style of public speaking had earned Barker the sobriquet of 'Squeaky'. At this moment, the Torpedomen on watch in the Forward Room were crowded around the watertight door leading into the Forward Battery and the wardroom. Chief Keller and his deck crew slapped their hands over their mouths to contain the laughter Squeaky's voice invoked. Keller watched Simon involuntarily blow his nose over his hand-covered mouth. Simon laughed so hard, snot exploded from his nostrils and rocketed across the room to land audibly on the door to the Officers' Head.

Secrets were impossible on boats. The entire crew knew Tunny's mission in less than five minutes of Barker's outburst. Except, that by the time the word had reached the After Room, the mission involved Tunny torpedoing every floating vessel in the harbor including the harbormaster's dinghy.

Browne calmed the XO's outburst with measured remarks.

"First, Mr. Barker, the mysterious freighter is CIA! They've been in before and know the harbor.

"Second, North Vietnamese sonar equipment and the personnel trained to operate it would be useless in that shallow environment.

"Finally, this is the Tunny. Nothing is impossible for this ship and crew. We've never shirked an assignment before and we're not about to start now! I want each of you to brief your men in detail after I announce the mission. We can afford no mistakes on this one. One final word, Gentlemen—never sell this crew short again. These are the best sailors in the world and they will follow each of you into the mouth of Neptune if you lead them. And I mean lead! Now sit down here and work out the operational details.

"COB, follow me to Control and I'll fill the crew in."

Browne and Vincent left the wardroom bound for Control. The remaining officers were left to brainstorm the operation. Various crewmen were invited in to complete the planning details; not the least of whom was Chief Sonarman Allen Leonard.

"Ears" Leonard was a tall gawky fellow with ears that protruded from his head at right angles. Ears looked for all the world like a taxicab with its doors open. He wore thick glasses and cropped his hair short on the sides and back. He had a receding jaw line, a protruding Adam's apple and acne. He was also a genius. At 28, he was the youngest Chief in Tunny. Scuttlebutt had it that he aced his Chief's exam. In fact, he had registered the highest score on the Chief Sonarman's exam since it had been revised after WWII. It was common knowledge aboard Tunny that Ears could hear a mouse fart. Not only that, he could tell the musical scale and key in which the offending rodent had flatulated. Obviously, Ears would be critical to the operation.

When O'Rourke asked Ears if it was possible for him to follow the freighter on sonar, his reply was direct.

"Sir, I've already listened to the tape once and that freighter's louder than the Boston Pops." Ears had a passion for classical music.

"Not only does it have a distinctive cavitation, but I can also hear their port side main shaft bearing beginning to fail. If that bearing fails while they're in port, we could be stuck there for quite a while. I could follow that bucket of bolts from Saigon!"

Barker brought in the watch-quarter-station bill and highlighted the names on the list assigned to bottoming operations. These crewmembers were picked for their particular expertise at assigned stations. O'Rourke was diving officer, Vincent was on the hydraulic manifold, Woods was on the trim manifold, etc. Each of these men had practiced expertise at each of these jobs and when Tunny went to bottoming operations, that expertise was required.

Turner pointed to the name assigned to the helm. "We have got to take Smith off the helm during bottoming. I caught him drinking gilly on watch. I think he's out of control with his drinking."

"OK," said Barker. "Who do you recommend to replace him?"

"I really like that kid, Berg. He's got a real feel for the old bucket and is conscientious as hell. He's been bugging the crap out of me for two days to qualify him in the Conn. I know he's new, but I trust him." That was good enough for Barker and the rest of Tunny's wardroom.

Barker said, "Anyone else we need to examine for this job?"

"Yes sir," said Mike. "I've been watching the Jackson kid on the stern planes. I think he can handle the job, but I need a few hours to work with him before I say for sure."

"When do you want to perform the training? Tonight?" asked Gary Barker.

"Yessir, while it's dark and you have the Conn. I want to see if he can anticipate trim changes while we are backing down."

Everyone in the wardroom knew Mike's concern. During normal operations when the boat was traveling forward while submerged, the bow planes controlled depth and the stern planes controlled dive angle. However, when reversing or backing down, the role of the planes was reversed. This meant that the planes operators had to monitor opposite gauges and the confusion was always dangerous. Practice and skill were essential qualities for planes operators during bottoming and un-bottoming operations.

"OK," the XO agreed. "We can also try Berg on the helm at the same time. That operation is also reversed during un-bottoming."

These were the only changes recommended from the regular bottoming crew. Browne, Turner, and Anderson completed the operational planning. The XO and O'Rourke called Simon and David to their new assignments. After a few hours training, Mike was assured David could handle the stern planes and Simon was competent on the helm. As always, Woods was on the trim manifold and Yeoman Hennessey manned the bow planes.

Two days later, the SS Jan Mayen, a freighter of Norwegian registry, was signaling with her fathometer at the rendezvous location. The Morse code signal for the letter "T", a single dash, was used as the signal. Normal fathometer transmissions were a single ping that echoed off the bottom. The use of a dash was not so unusual as to draw attention to the freighter. Tunny picked up the signal on passive sonar and followed it to the rendezvous point.

It was 2330 hours local time when Tunny surfaced astern of the Jan Mayen and contacted her by signal lamp. They were 50 miles east of Haiphong in the midst of the hostile waters of The Gulf of Tonkin. The Navy had designated this area of the Tonkin Gulf "Yankee Station." The waters off South Vietnam were designated "Rebel Station."

Neither vessel had armament greater than a 50-caliber machine gun. They relied solely on stealth and secrecy to protect them. Thankfully, the moon had set and the night was a dark as the devil's soul.

The Jan Mayen's captain put a small boat in the water and transited to the Tunny. Tunny had kept her main deck low to the water to reduce her radar profile, so it was with ease that the one-legged Captain of the freighter boarded the submarine. In spite of the cloak of secrecy, formalities were observed and the 1MC announced the arrival of the freighter's skipper, "Jan Mayen—arriving!"

In the wardroom, preparations for the secret penetration of Haiphong were finalized.

"Captain Browne," said LTJG Oldham, "It is my honor to introduce you to Commandant Eric Skein, master of the Norwegian freighter Jan Mayen."

Skein extended his hand in the traditional Western gesture of friendship. "Welcome aboard, sir," said Browne. They shook hands warmly as only men charged with command responsibility could understand.

"Captain, how do you propose to follow Jan Mayen into the harbor?" queried Skein. They sat at the wardroom table with the charts on display in front of them. "These charts are 40 years old and of French origin. The Viet Minh have altered the harbor a great deal since these were published." Skein spoke with in a heavy Scandinavian accent and with the confidence of one who was comfortable with authority.

"I have much more current charts that include the latest in your country's air reconnaissance. I have been instructed to provide them for your use. But I'm not sure you will need them since you propose to follow Jan Mayen close astern into Haiphong. Just how close do you plan to follow?"

"My sonarman says he can follow you at 200 yards. He feels this is a comfortable distance," replied Browne.

"Not acceptable!" scoffed Skein. "You must get within 100 yards if you expect to get past the submarine nets before they close in our wake."

"100 yards! I don't think that's possible, Captain! If you come to a sudden stop or make a sudden turn, we'll run right up your shaft alleys before you can say 'Yumpin' Yimminy'!" The fake accent from Barker brought a laugh from everyone in the wardroom, including Captain Skein.

Once the laughter had subsided, Skein said, "You'll just have to trust us not to make sudden course changes. You don't have a choice if you want to make a success of this operation. And I don't intend to have myself and my crew shot as spies, do you understand?"

"What have I told you, XO, about selling this crew short? There is nothing Tunny can't accomplish with the proper leadership," said Bill Browne. "Captain Skein, what's your plan?"

In his Norwegian-accented English, Eric Skein explained the details of the planned Haiphong harbor intrusion by the USS Tunny. Jan Mayen would maintain a constant speed of four knots from the time the harbormaster boarded until she cleared all the harbor obstructions. Tunny would have to maintain an equal speed to avoid being trapped in the sub netting. The sub nets were lowered to allow access for deep draft vessels like Jan Mayen. They were immediately raised once the vessels cleared them. However, it took about five minutes for the slack to be taken out of the cable from which the nets were attached. This five-minute window was all Tunny had to clear the nets or become hopelessly entangled. The minefields would be defeated by staying in Jan Mayen's wake at the uncomfortable distance of 100 yards.

Browne would use the periscope to set the 100-yard interval initially. Then it would be necessary to lower the periscope to avoid detection on harbor radar. From then on, the interval and course would be determined by passive sonar. Ears Leonard would become the conning officer and his sense of hearing would determine the fate of the assigned mission. Tunny would essentially be in command of a 28 year old, pimple-faced Chief Sonarman during the most challenging mission of her illustrious career.

Once in the harbor and past the obstacles, Jan Mayen would send two quick pings on her fathometer to inform Tunny to break off and bottom at a designated vantage point. This vantage point was out of the main channel, but it provided a clear view of the harbor, the vessels in port and any harbor patrol boats. It also allowed Tunny to mask its snorkel induction mast among other more conspicuous radar targets. Tunny would have to raise the snorkel induction mast after dark to allow fresh air into the pressure hull. Anderson and his UDT team would reconnoiter ashore every night to accomplish mapping and other hydrographic activities. Once Jan Mayen was off-loaded, she would signal with her fathometer and Tunny would take station astern of her for the harbor egress.

"What is the depth of the main channel, Captain Skein?" asked O'Rourke.

"I don't believe that should present you with a problem," replied Skien. "The last time we were here, we took depth readings all the way in. The harbor at its shallowest is 80 feet and that was at the sub netting."

"OK, we can handle that. Where is your assigned berth…just in case we need to contact you?" asked Turner.

Skein was quick to answer, "We won't know that until we take on the harbor pilot. The Russians have so many ships in this port that it is most congested. To avoid a long stay, however, we are loaded with perishable foodstuffs this time. That should guarantee us a dockside berth and facilitated off-loading…one or two days at the most in port."

At this juncture, coordinates were exchanged and timepieces were synchronized. Jan Mayen ascended to his small boat and returned to his ship. Further detailed planning continued in the wardroom with Ears Leonard and Chief Vincent in attendance.

"Sir, did you mention the main bearing on the port shaft to the Captain of Jan Mayer?" asked Chief Leonard.

"Damn, I knew there was something we forgot!" said Bill Browne under his breath.

Chapter Eleven

Haiphong

Everything was proceeding as planned. Leonard's special talent on the passive sonar kept Tunny close astern of the SS Jan Mayer and she cleared the submarine net with about 10 seconds to spare. Once inside the harbor, Tunny was forced to scramble to get back in trim. The density differences between seawater and the brackish water of the river mouth, as well as the water temperature, required O'Rourke to re-trim ship expeditiously.

Jackson and Hennessey responded rapidly on the planes to prevent Tunny from broaching or exposing the sail above water. They had waited until well after the moon had set to enter the harbor. The cloak of night increased the odds against their detection.

They were now approaching their appointed bottoming station. Bill Browne raised the small scope to get a position fix. A radio antennae attached to the small periscope received signals from LORAN C that allowed Turner and Smith to determine their location.

O'Rourke and his bottoming crew eased Tunny into the soft mud of the river bottom about 0415. The strain had taken its toll on the crew. Most, however, were just physically exhausted. Browne set the regular sea watch and had the snorkel induction mast raised to ventilate the boat. The bottoming crew had been on watch for nine straight hours without relief. They were given special treatment in the crews' mess and assigned to their bunks until further notice. The ingress operation had been flawless. Browne had never been more proud of his crew. He ordered "dead quiet" set and sought the relief of his stateroom.

About 0605, he was awakened by Hennessey. He recognized a four-degree list to starboard as he rubbed the sleep from his eyes and returned to Control. He noticed the look of concern on Barker's face.

"What's the problem, Gary?" he said.

"Sir, the tide's going out. If it ebbs much further, we'll be a sittin' duck! We gotta move!"

Browne did not let his concern enter his voice. He spoke quietly so as to defeat any panic the XO could have aroused.

"LT Barker, how could we overlook something as elementary as the tide? Where are the tide charts for this area—didn't anyone consult them before we picked this spot to bottom?"

Barker was suddenly calmed by his Captain's even-tempered response.

"Yessir. That's one of the first things we checked. But they're wrong, sir. I've been checking and double-checking for the last hour. Somehow, when translating from the French, someone screwed up! The worst part is that the sun's coming up now and we gotta move further into the channel or risk detection. I recommend setting the bottoming watch so we can re-position into deeper waters."

"Very well!" Browne grabbed the microphone for the 1MC. "Now hear this! Now hear this! All hands! Set the bottoming watch! Set the bottoming watch!"

Sleep-deprived sailors scrambled from their racks to don hastily discarded dungarees and hurried to their assigned posts. They knew instinctively that something was wrong. Even the newest crewmembers could feel the tension in the air. It took less than 90 seconds for the watch to be manned and ready. Adrenaline was pumping through every artery in Tunny and that hormone drove the lethargy from their bodies.

O'Rourke appeared at his station with his shirt unbuttoned and his shoes untied. He quickly finished dressing on watch. "What's up, Sir?"

"The tide's ebbing and we may be exposed if we don't move to deeper waters. Get everything ready to move. I'll be in the Conn." Browne climbed the ladder into the Conning tower and raised the #1 periscope. "OK, Mike, back us outta here!"

Now began a delicate balancing act with nature. The first thing

Mike needed to do was get Tunny's screws out of the mud. This was accomplished by bleeding high-pressure air into numbers 6A&B main ballast tanks, the ballast tanks closest to Tunny's stern. His first command was to operate all main vents to ascertain the ballast tanks were completely flooded. Then he ordered all main vents shut. "Commence blowing 6A&B main ballast tanks."

Eddie Rance cracked the valves on the air manifold that sent 600 PSI air to the after ballast tanks. Tunny began to right herself from the slight starboard list.

"Secure the blow!" Tunny began to take on a down angle as her stern rose from the muddy river bottom. "All back dead slow! Three degree down angle!"

"Bow planes at three degrees down, sir" said Hennessey.

"You're coming up too fast, Mike! Open the vents!" Bill Browne was watching through the periscope and his perspective told him the scope was more than ten feet out of the water.

"All back one third! Open all main vents!" ordered Mike.

Simon, on the helm, rang up all back one third and got an immediate response from Maneuvering. "Answers all back one third, sir. Rudder is amidships, sir!" Simon volunteered.

At the same time chief Vincent opened the vent valves to release the air from the ballast tanks. Tunny settled back to an even keel.

"Zero angle on the stern planes. Maintain five five feet!"

Jackson responded and brought the stern planes to zero degrees. Because Tunny was backing, he was controlling Tunny's depth while Hennessey watched the inclinometer. Tunny's depth gauge read 50 feet when she was bottomed. Jackson caught Mike's error and shook his head in the negative. O'Rourke knew immediately why he had chosen Jackson for this assignment. He kept a cool head and still managed to cover the diving officer's ass.

"Going to five-five feet, sir," responded David. He put about one degree down angle on the stern planes as Tunny righted herself and pulled away from the river bottom.

It was at about this time that the Browne burst into uncontrolled laughter in the Conn. He had been watching Tunny's progress through the periscope in the dim predawn light. A civilian fishing fleet had put out on the river to secure their morning catch. All the vessels in the fleet were one-outrigger canoes, each equipped

81

with a Coleman lantern to provide lighting. The fishermen cast their nets off the clean side of their canoes and waited for them to fill with the river's scaly bounty.

One unfortunate soul had cast his net over Tunny. As the submarine began to move toward the channel, the fisherman perceived a steady tug on his net. He frantically began to pull it back aboard his canoe in a hand-over-hand struggle. When Tunny picked up speed and the periscope began to make a wake, the hapless riverman's face struck a terrified pose. Without hesitation, he began to jettison his nets to free himself from the monster that had caught him. Bill Browne could not control his mirth. Tears welled up in his eyes and he couldn't catch his breath to speak.

Harvey Turner responded to Bill's gestures to peer through the scope. It took him less than 10 seconds to recognize what had caused the Skipper's outburst of laughter. Harvey also succumbed to the humor of the situation. He nearly fell to the Conning Tower deck in uncontrolled amusement.

O'Rourke and the rest of the crew on bottoming stations were bewildered by the reactions of their commanding officer and his navigator. Tunny was in a serious situation, the consequences of which were dire. To suddenly have the leadership break into hilarity was, at the least, disconcerting. But the high tension was relieved and the laughter was contagious. Soon everyone in the Conn and in Control was laughing. Only two knew the origin of humor, but these two drew the rest of the crew into their comedy even without understanding the joke.

"All stop!" said Browne through his laughter.

Simon replied and rang up all stop on the repeater. "Answers all stop, sir."

Tunny settled back into the mud of the river bottom. Her depth gauge now read 56 feet depth to keel. The rising tide would eventually drown her periscope and she would have to move again, but for now she was safe at this depth. She could wait for nightfall and the safety of darkness to find a better location. In the meantime, Gary Barker had solved the mystery of the French tidal charts. They had apparently been compiled during a period of flood years. By subtracting a constant 5 feet from the chart readings, he could compensate for the inaccuracy.

Browne and Turner described the view through the periscope to those below and the laughter was renewed again; this time the entire crew got to participate.

The problem now was to communicate Tunny's new location to the Jan Mayen. LT Anderson and his UDT crew volunteered to approach the freighter, board her under cover of darkness, and provide the new information to Captain Eric Skein. Preparations were made for a deployment of frogmen that next night.

Chapter Twelve

Launch

Because of the river's current, murky water conditions and complete darkness, this exercise would be very complicated. Tunny would have to surface to accomplish the UDT launch. Then it would be necessary for the ship's deck gang to open the boat lockers, release the IBS's (a Navy acronym for "inflatable boats, small") from the lockers, secure them to Tunny's mooring cleats, and load the frogmen's gear into the boats. All this was to be accomplished in the dark with vision reduced to less than ten feet.

The Skipper said, "No problem, Anderson. Get your men ready for launch."

Browne determined that he could keep Tunny's silhouette low by only exposing about 12 inches of freeboard. In the dark, Tunny's profile disappeared into the opposite bank, so detection from the Haiphong bank of the Red River was not likely. However, someone on the opposite bank could easily see the submarine outlined against the lights of the city. They would have to be quick and efficient to reduce the probability of the enemy sighting them.

The low profile would, however, cause flooding in the hangar deck bilge. This flooding would again change Tunny's trim characteristics and require pumping before she could submerge.

Anderson assembled his team in the hangar, explained the situation and had them prepare for a surface launch. They wouldn't need wet suits, goggles or swim fins normally used when Tunny served as a submerged launch platform. This time they would need to be armed, however.

Browne took one last look around through the scope before he brought Tunny up slowly. The ballast tank blow was controlled and measured so as to not empty the tanks completely. The deck gang was assembled in the hangar with the tools required to open the after deck boat lockers, release and inflate the IBS's. The .50 caliber gun crews were also in attendance. There were two .50 mounts on Tunny's after deck and two more on the bridge. The bridge gun crews were assembled in the Forward Room. The UDT team would not appear on deck until the guns were mounted and the IBS's launched and secured to bollards provided on the superstructure.

"Crack the hatch!" was Browne's command to Snuffy standing by the Conning Tower hatch. Snuffy spun the wheel on the hatch counter-clockwise and undogged the hatch to the bridge. The hiss of pressurized air escaped Tunny instantly. Everyone on board felt the sudden drop to atmospheric pressure on their eardrums. Most equalized the inner ear pressure by locking and unlocking their jaws. Some had to grab their noses and blow to clear their Eustachian tubes.

Snuffy climbed to the bridge first, carrying sound-powered phones and other necessary communication equipment. The lookouts followed Snuffy and assumed their lookout stations while Snuffy activated the phones and annunciators. The lookouts had swept the horizon once even before the Old Man made it to the bridge. Visual contacts were relayed to the Captain in muffled tones and confirmed by the Officer of the Deck, XO Gary Barker.

Browne confirmed the all clear with Harvey Turner, who was on the periscope in the Conning Tower. The ship's Navigator always manned the scope during surface operations.

"Open the hangar door and launch the IBS's!" Browne barked to Snuffy, who was on the sound-powered phones.

The high pitched squeal of hydraulic fluid under pressure came from the huge hydraulic rams used to raise the immense hangar door. The door cracked open and brackish river water flooded the bilge as the pneumatic rams raised and locked the launch deck into place aft of the hangar.

Even before the hangar door was completely open, the deck gang sprang into action. They hustled out on the after deck with ratchet wrenches and flashlights covered with red lenses. Mike O'Rourke and Chief Keller participated in the operation of the boat launch. One of the crew appeared with a flexible air hose and began to "top off" the air pressure in the IBS's while those ready for launch were pushed off the side and secured to the mooring cleats in the deck.

When four boats were in the water, the UDT Team appeared with their gear to board. Because Browne had used a controlled blow, there was less than 12 inches of freeboard. This maneuver made boarding easy and swift. Oars were the last item produced from the boat lockers. They would be needed once the UDT Team got close to Jan Mayen. Most of the transit could be made using the ultra-silent outboard engines designed specially for this use. Roger Roads and Tim Lang joined the UDT team in the boats to secure the IBS's once they reached the Jan Mayen.

Before Tunny began submergence operations, communications and sonar vectoring were tested for operation. The mission would fail were the UDT unable to communicate with Tunny or to find their way home.

Bill Browne took one last sweep of the horizon through his glasses. Nothing appeared unusual in the murk of midnight that surrounded Tunny in her makeshift berth on the Red River.

Several hundred yards away, hiding in the dense underbrush on the south bank of the Red, stood Major Duk Lu of the North Vietnamese Army (NVA). Strange tales of sea serpents that stole fishing nets from unsuspecting fishermen had called him to the area. His binoculars were focused on the strange looking silhouette framed against the lights of Haiphong. It had to be a submarine, he reasoned. But from what nation? He knew Russia and China had underwater craft that operated in the harbor. Could this be one of theirs? It almost had to be because no other foreign vessel could clear the submarine defenses at the mouth of the Red without detection—or could they?

He hurried to his Japanese-built command car, anxious to report his sighting to his superiors across the river. Sinking or capturing a US Navy submarine would be a great honor for himself and his family. Perhaps he could get increased food rations because of this discovery.

Chapter Thirteen

Discovery

Hours after the departure of Anderson and his UDT crew and while Tunny still rested on the bottom of the Red River, Chief Vincent began to worry.

"We gotta blow 'em, sir. They're overflowing onto the After Battery deck. If that salt water gets into the battery well, we'll have hell to pay!"

Browne knew he was right. The sanitary tanks hadn't been blown since entering the harbor. Even with the showers secured, human bodily functions required the use of the heads. Now the tank was full and all the vent valves had to be shut to prevent salt water from entering the battery well bilge. Should this happen, a chemical reaction would take place, producing chlorine gas from the battery acid. Although chlorine gas is odorless, colorless and tasteless, it is very deadly.

"OK, COB. But let me have a look around before we send a signal to the enemy as to our location. If it's all clear, I'll order the tank blown."

"One more thing, Cap'n. Chief Gordon says we need run one of the diesels to charge the battery and ventilate the boat. We haven't been able to strike a match for about eight hours."

Bill knew the air was foul. His head was exploding from the headache he always experienced when the CO_2 content inside the boat exceeded a safe level. Even with the snorkel induction mast raised, they could not draw enough fresh air into the boat to displace the heavier carbon dioxide. The inconvenience to the smokers on board was minor compared to the effects of the CO_2 pollution.

Browne raised the scope and did a 360-degree scan three times. The moon was shining bright and its reflection provided a moon path straight to the harbor entrance. He saw nothing that appeared threatening and so ordered the sanitary tank evacuated and a battery charge begun.

Within minutes, fresh air was pouring into Tunny through the snorkel induction mast. He saw, through the scope, the engine exhaust bubbling up from under the diffusion plate that covered the snorkel exhaust mast. The snorkel exhaust mast opening was below the surface of the water. Exhaust backpressure kept the engines from flooding and the exhaust was water-soluble. This feature lessened the chance of visual detection.

Just then he watched as the debris from Sanitary surfaced. The gases from Sanitary were sucked back into Tunny through the induction mast. He could hear the snipes in the Engine Room bitching already.

"Just where is Anderson and his team?" he wondered.

Colonel Dak of the NVA, who'd just arrived in the area, heard Tunny's operations before they could make visual contact. Sound travels well across water, but the direction from which it came was difficult to discern. Major Lu had used dead reckoning to report the previous night's sighting. A breeze ruffled the surface of the usually placid river and made visual contact difficult. But after some concentrated effort, Dak saw the engine exhaust bubbles and the sanitary tank emissions surfacing.

Colonel Dak had been sent by high command to verify Lu's sighting and confirm the presence of a hostile visitor. High command had determined that no Russian or Chinese submersibles were in the harbor at this time. The last Russian sub had left Haiphong more than a week ago. Dak had run across the filthy Russians in town. They all smelled of diesel fuel and sweat. Their sanitary habits were primitive and their sexual desires insatiable. When they weren't drunk on rice wine, they were fornicating with the prostitutes that inhabited the many bars along the harbor front.

Their rubles were welcomed, however, so they were tolerated as allies. The alliance between the highly religious Vietnamese and atheistic Russians was a fragile one. But the Russians supplied much needed war material and foodstuffs. Dak reasoned they would have to tolerate the uncivilized Cossacks until they settled the conflict with the equally barbaric Americans.

Dak set up a transit and determined the exact location of the suspicious surface activity. Once this had been verified three times, he turned the crank on an ancient Russian radio transmitter. He proceeded to send the coordinates to the North Vietnamese harbor patrol for investigation. They promised they would dispatch a patrol craft at dawn.

Chapter Fourteen

Jan Mayen

It took a couple of hours for the UDT to transit the harbor to the unloading docks. The Jan Mayen was not difficult to find, even at night. Her cargo was in the process of being offloaded. This required abundant lighting for the operation of the gantry cranes and cargo netting. The perishable nature of the cargo forced the dock master to bring Jan Mayen alongside a pier with ready access to refrigerated storage.

The small, silent outboard engines were used to make most of the UDT's harbor transit. But even these quiet machines were secured upon approaching the dock area. Anderson had no intention of alerting the crew of the Mayen to their arrival. Anderson assigned Roads and Lang to remain with the IBS's and to hide with them under the pier.

Using grappling hooks and hand lines, the frogmen boarded the freighter from outboard and found temporary shelter under one of her life rafts. None of the Norwegian crew was in sight.

"Strange," thought Anderson. The UDT team, in practiced stealth, spread out about the freighter. Each team member had an assigned area of the ship to reconnoiter. Anderson headed for the bridge and Captain's Quarters with Petty Officer Chambers. Chambers was the sniper in Team 12.

They ascended the ladder to the poop deck, just aft of the bridge; still none of the crew were discovered. But standing watch at the gangway was an NVA private armed with an AK47. Loud voices were now heard in Captain Skein's stateroom. The voice was definitely Vietnamese speaking Oxford English. Apparently this was the only language Skein and his inquisitor had in common.

Peering through the outboard porthole into Skein's cabin, Anderson saw that Skein and his first mate were trussed to chairs back-to-back to each other. An NVA major stood over Skein and was demanding the location of the "Yankee intruders."

"We know they are here. We have reports from a fisherman who had his nets stolen," said the major. "Your denials are useless. We will find the intruders with or without your help. Your continued lies will only serve to work further hardships on your crew."

Skein's face was bloody and swollen. His nose was obviously broken and he was bleeding from his left ear. Two teeth were missing. "I do not lie, major. The presence of intruders, as you call them, is news to me—and my crew. Your invasion of this ship is against international law and your treatment of my crew is against the laws of the sea. Further disregard for these laws will result in an international reaction against you and your country." Skein was bluffing and doing an admirable job of the act, in spite of the torture to which he was being subjected.

The major unholstered his Chinese pistol, placed the barrel on Skein's right shoulder and discharged a round directly into the back of the First Mate's head. The entry wound was small, but the bullet exited from the unsuspecting officer's forehead, taking a large section of the skull with it. The dead man's pulverized cranial material splattered the bulkhead and leaked from his slumping head onto his lap.

Captain Skein's right eardrum was broken so he barely heard himself scream in despair for his shipmate. Norwegian curse words came from his mouth in rapid unrestraint. He looked into his antagonist's eyes and saw his own imminent death. The pistol was being leveled on Skein's forehead just as the 9mm slug from Anderson's silenced Berretta blew the major's head apart. Instinctive muscle reaction caused the body to squeeze the trigger of the pistol, but the round flew wild into the overhead and he was propelled across the compartment into the opposite bulkhead. The major's body then slumped to the deck.

Skein's eyes were wide with fright and the added adrenaline caused him to work against his restraints and cut his wrists. Just then

Anderson appeared at the portside doorway with PO Chambers. "Chambers! Get to the fair weather bridge and assemble the team! We gotta get out o' here!" ordered Anderson.

"No! No!" yelled Skein. "They have my crew in a warehouse on the pier. They will kill them, just like they did poor Michael, here!"

"Where the fuck are they?" shouted Anderson. "We can get them back aboard and take this old tub outta here! Are there any more NVA aboard?"

Skein, cut from his restraints, wiped the blood from his face with his sleeve. "This son-of-a-bitch and his asshole sentry are the only ones on Mayen," he said. He staggered to the starboard side of the bridge and pointed to a large storehouse just opposite the Mayen's gangway. "The rest are in there. That's where I saw the Colonel take my crew."

Just then the NVA sentry at the Mayen's gangplank clutched his face as he fell over the side. His head hit a bollard on the pier as he fell into the harbor. The only noise came from his AK47 as it fell to the deck. Chambers had anticipated the need for a clear passage to the warehouse. His next shot killed the gantry crane operator offloading from the Mayen's cargo hold. The crane came to a halt in mid-movement, the load swaying recklessly from the sudden stop.

Using hand signals, Anderson assembled his team on the bridge. "Captain, we've got to get the hell out of here right now!"

"I'll need some help launching the small craft," replied Skein. "Do any of your team have small boat experience?"

Anderson gestured to one of his team members, "Get those two sailors out from under the pier and have them report to the Captain."

Then to Skein, "Have them launch a small boat you have on board. Make sure the boat has enough room for your crew and my Team. I'll have your crew on the pier within 30 minutes."

Then he spoke to the sniper and his UDT Team, "Chambers— stay on the flying bridge and provide cover. The rest of you follow me."

Chapter Fifteen

Change of Plans

Roger and Tim heard the thud of the sentry's AK47 and looked up just in time to catch a view of his body as it cascaded into the water. He floated face up and his lower jaw was missing.

They sensed, rather than heard; the UDT team leave Mayen in the direction of the warehouse. One of the UDT team startled them when he called to them from the pier supports above and behind them.

"Bring those rubber boats around to outboard and prepare to take on passengers. The shit's hit the fan here and we need to get back to Tunny ASAP! We'll signal with two flashes from the red lens when we are ready to board. In the meantime, don't let anybody else off the Mayen to outboard. Are you guys armed?"

"I don't know," said Tim. "What's in this here plastic box?"

"Should be two 45's and a couple of grenades. Can you handle those weapons?"

"Yessir! How long you gonna be?" asked Roger.

"Don't know! But don't leave without us! You're our only way out and we'll have company with us." He disappeared as mysteriously as he had materialized.

Tim and Roger carefully maneuvered the small boats around the bow of Mayen and into position on her outboard side where the boarding party had climbed aboard. They took their time and made the move without any noise.

Once they arrived, Tim had an idea. "Hey, Roger, let's go up there and lower the Jacob's ladder. That will make it a lot easier for the UDT to get in the boats."

"I don't think we should, Tim! Besides, I'm not going up that rope into God know what kind of trouble!" Roger's eyes were wide open and he was visibly shaken by this unexpected turn of events.

Tim didn't even stop to argue. He grabbed the nearest climbing rope and began to scale the side of Mayen. He was on deck and at the davit that lowered the Jacob's ladder in less than thirty seconds. He studied the lowering mechanism for a couple of minutes and then engaged the winch. A grinding, clanking sound broke the night stillness as the Ladder began to descend from Mayen's main deck.

Chambers, perched high on the flying bridge in his position as sniper, heard the noise and moved to the outboard side of the flying bridge to ascertain the cause. He saw only the silhouette of someone lowering the Jacob's ladder. As far as he knew, there were no friend-lies left on Mayen. He viewed the target through his scope, put the crosshairs on his head and squeezed off his shot.

Meanwhile, the ladder got hung up in the wire rope railing on Mayen's forward deck. Tim leaned over to free it from the obstruc-tion. This movement saved his life. The sniper's bullet slammed into the railing, knocking a fragment of steel loose from a post. This steel projectile ricocheted up and caught Tim in the neck. He toppled backward onto the deck and then slowly rolled over the side of Mayen.

Meanwhile, in the warehouse, Anderson and the frogmen searched for the crew of Mayen. They heard noises coming from a second story loft of the warehouse and moved toward the loft in standard cover formation. Sacks of grain and wooden crates were stored fifteen feet high on the floor of the warehouse, leaving only narrow aisles between the stacks. Six of the team climbed to the top of the stored material and began scouting ahead for the remainder of the team who were advancing through the aisles.

The noises became clearly distinguishable voices as the neared the sound. Some of the voices were speaking Vietnamese. These voices were loud and demanding. They were answered by more measured voices with a Scandinavian accent. Though neither lan-guage was understood by the UDT, it was obvious that an interro-gation of the Mayen crew was being conducted.

Using hand signals, the frogmen surrounded the office where the interrogation was underway. Anderson was the first to break through the flimsy balsa wood door to the office. The two NVA inquisitors were dead from headshots within five seconds. Anderson's crew untied the 15 Mayen crew members in the room. "Are there any more of you guys in here?" asked Anderson.

"They kept the Captain and the First Mate on board," replied one of the Mayen crew.

"We already have them. Let's clear this area before we have any more guests." Anderson checked the two bodies for intelligence. One had a handwritten note in his tunic pocket. It appeared to have been signed by someone of authority in the NVA. He stuffed the note inside his shirt. There was nothing else of interest, just a few North Vietnamese bills and coins, a set of keys and a pack of cigarettes. Anderson left the cigarettes, but commandeered a lighter and the money as spoils of war.

He was the last to leave the warehouse and cross the gangplank back into Mayen. He began making his way to the flying bridge when he saw the muzzle flash from Chambers' .247mm sniper rifle. He caught a glimpse of Tim's body just before it fell into the river. He recognized Chambers' victim as one of the Tunny sailors attached to his reconnaissance party.

"Chambers! Hold your fire! That's our man!" Anderson hollered. The rest of the UDT Team and the Mayen's crew were headed outboard and couldn't see what had just happened to Tim.

From below in the IBS's, Roger watched in stunned horror as Tim teetered just under the rail. Tim looked down at Roger and tried to ask for help, but the shrapnel was lodged against his voice box. Tim fell into the river within easy reach of Roger. He reached up and tried to grasp one of the boarding ropes on the most inboard IBS. His hand missed the rope and he began to slip under the water. Roger grabbed at Tim, but missed him. He began to scream Tim's name.

Anderson landed in the river feet first just behind Tim and grasped him around the chest. With his free hand, he caught the boarding rope on the nearest IBS and began to push Tim into the boat.

The Jacob's ladder had lowered itself entirely and the wench mechanism was banging against the stops. Someone on deck switched the motor off. The Mayen crew, Captain Skein and the frogmen of UDT Team 12 lowered the Captain's launch and took the rubber boats in tow. Tim received first aid from the hospital corpsman assigned to Team 12. The wound was superficial, but it caused swelling that blocked Tim's voice box. He stared at Roger the entire trip back to Tunny.

Chapter Sixteen

Trapped

Team 12 approached the location with caution. From what they had learned on Mayen, they could be heading right into a trap. Anderson was relieved to hear a response on his radio receiver from Captain Browne. Using the night vision feature on the small periscope, Browne vectored the frogmen toward him. He caught sight of them at 400 yards and was surprised to see the Captain's launch from the Mayen. At 200 yards, he told Anderson to hold his position while Tunny surfaced.

Again, Browne controlled the ballast tank blow so as to keep Tunny low in the water—only 12 inches of freeboard. Once aboard, Tim was rushed below and examined by the ship's Corpsman. The steel fragment was removed, but swelling around the wound continued to press against his vocal cords, rendering him speechless. Captain Skein was also examined. He was missing some teeth and his nose was broken. He also had several scalp wounds and both his eardrums were broken. He would not, however, be kept from the wardroom where there was a strategic meeting taking place.

Anderson reported to Browne. "We gotta get outta here tonight, sir! They know you are here. They will probably send someone out for you as soon as it is light." They checked their watches. It was 0400—dawn in less than two hours.

"Why don't we just move again? I don't think they can find us, 'cause they don't seem to have serviceable sonar equipment. Even if they do, finding us while we are bottomed will be next to impossible."

Browne was thinking out loud—bouncing ideas off the wardroom bulkheads for his staff to evaluate.

Gary Barker agreed with the Skipper. "We could even move across the river and bottom in the harbor."

O'Rourke objected. "Our mission wasn't to become a hazard to navigation by obstructing the channel! I say we move out. Let Ears and his crew find a new escort and clear the harbor for the open sea."

Then Captain Skein spoke. "You can't leave the Mayen moored to the dock for them to search. There is too much sensitive material on board and the propensity for an international incident will endanger Norway's neutrality and any future joint covert operations. We must destroy the Mayen within the next hour or they will have the evidence they need to condemn Norway in the United Nations!"

Browne took over. "He's right! XO—you have the good Captain here draw you a compartment-by-compartment diagram of Mayen below the waterline.

"Mike—you go forward and load all the forward tubes with Mark 37's. I'll give you depth settings from the Conn.

"COB—set the bottoming watch! Let's move!"

COB grabbed the 1MC microphone from the wardroom bulkhead and pressed the talk key: "Now hear this! Now hear this! Set the Bottoming watch! Set the Bottoming watch!"

The crew scrambled to their watch stations and prepared to take Tunny out into the channel. Tim tried to man his watch station, but the corpsman restrained him. Tim's blood loss, though not critical, left him light headed. The image of Roger's terrified face kept appearing in his mind's eye. Tim had an uneasy feeling about Roger. Had he sensed uncontrolled fear in his shipmate?

Tunny slipped easily from the bottom and backed out into the rivers current. Browne maneuvered her around until she pointed upriver. Mike kept her depth at 59 feet—just enough room for the big periscope to break the surface. Using the DRT, Snuffy, Skein and LT Turner navigated Tunny toward the port and the awaiting Jan Mayen.

At 0500, Tunny was 600 yards from the Mayen and was lined up for a broadside shot with her torpedoes. A plan had been forming in Browne's mind. He was now ready to share it with the others in the Conning Tower.

"We'll use only the Mark 37 torpedoes to sink the Mayen. They don't leave the wake the M14's do and maybe the NVA will think they are under an air raid. We will use two fish to sink the Mayen and set the other two fish to explode under the dock and warehouse. Skein, where are the Mayen's fuel bunkers? Show me through the 'scope here!"

Captain Skein peered through Tunny's periscope at his ship. He knew he was abetting in her destruction and he felt a twinge of conscience when he saw her tied innocently to the dock. He thought of his First Mate, Michael, lying dead on the deck of her bridge. What would he say to Michael's wife and family? How could he tell them he had deliberately destroyed their loved ones remains along with the ship he served and loved?

He put the cross hairs of the scope on Mayen's main fuel tank and said a silent prayer for his ship and his Mate. "There—about 50 feet aft of the bridge. The tanks are all below the waterline." With that he turned the scope over to Browne.

At the scope, Browne lined up the target. "Range—Mark!"

"560 yards!" was Turner's reply.

"Bearing—Mark!"

"174 degrees!"

It was like shooting fish in a barrel. "Fire one!"

"One's away, sir!"

"Fire Two!"

Because the range was so close, the first fish crashed into Mayen even before the second torpedo could be launched. "Two's away, sir!"

Browne began to line up on the pier. "Here's the second firing solution. Range—Mark!"

"600 yards!" Turner was clicking the solution off quickly now for input into the third Mk37 torpedo.

"Bearing—Mark!" The second fish struck the Mayen. A fireball ascended into the night sky, illuminating the entire harbor. The Mayen was burning and she began to list to port. Fuel oil from her fuel bunkers leaked into the river and spread the fire to other ships and port facilities as it followed the current down river..

"160 degrees, sir. Tube three is ready."

"Fire three!"

"Three's away, sir!" For the third time, Tunny shuddered as the electric torpedo swam out of the tube.

Browne was watching the fuel oil fire when the third fish

slammed into the pier forward of the burning Jan Mayen. He saw bodies silhouetted against the backdrop of the explosion fly into the air. Then, two hundred yards down river, anti-aircraft artillery (AAA) swung into action. Bursts of explosives were propelled skyward at an invisible, silent target.

Browne once more adjusted his scope. He focused the crosshairs just below the muzzle blasts of the AAA. "Bearing—Mark!"

"175 degrees, sir!"

"Range—Mark!"

"1200 yards!"

Turner sent the firing solution to the last Mk37 torpedo in the forward tubes. "Make this one count, Harvey! Fire four!"

"Four's away, sir!"

Browne watched with morbid fascination as his missile sped toward his chosen target. He almost wished he had used one of the Mk14's on this run. He could have seen the trail of steam left in the wake of the weapon. In a moment, the fish exploded under the AAA battery. It had apparently been mounted on one of the North Vietnamese Navy's small harbor patrol craft. The torpedo's explosion began to cook off the stored ammunition for the AAA gun. Several secondary explosions resulted from the other harbor patrol craft moored together in the same landing area.

The light from the Mayen's burning oil now blinded the night vision apparatus in the periscope. Browne switched to daylight vision and swung around to observe the flaming freighter. The burning oil was only a few yards for Tunny's scope.

"Down scope! Dive, Mike! Put her on the bottom!"

Mike instinctively checked the fathometer reading before instructing the planesmen and helmsman. The bottom was at 150 feet. Rather than driving Tunny to the bottom, he decided to simply let her settle softly into the mud.

"Flood auxiliaries from sea! Flood forward trim! Flood after trim!"

These instructions were for Woodsey on the trim manifold. Jim began working the trim manifold valves with his manual valve handle. He repeated all of Mike's instructions and began flooding Tunny's trim tanks with water from the Red River. The depth gauge began reacting immediately. Because forward trim was flooded before the after trim tank, Tunny took on a shallow down angle until her bow nudged into the bottom of the river. Tunny's stern settled down only a second later.

Mike reported, "Sir, we are on the bottom. Depth to keel reads 159 feet."

Browne acknowledged Mike and then said, "All Right, gentlemen. Let's see if we can pick up an escort out of here. Harvey, get me sonar on the phone."

Turner dialed the sound-powered phone indicator to the correct setting for the sonar room. He spun the handle on the side and waited for a response.

The bottoming watch was on the headset already. He simply keyed his mic and responded to LT Turner's call. "Sonar!"

"Put Ears on the phone—the Captain wants to talk to him."

Turner handed the phone to Browne. "Ears?"

"Aye, Sir."

"Ears! Get me a ride outta this place, quickly. Find me someone leaving so we can follow them down river and out to sea!"

"Yessir, but what about the Jan Mayen? Can't we follow her out?" queried Ears.

"No, Ears, she's gone." Browne glanced across the narrow compartment at Skein. He could only empathize with his fellow commander. The look on Skein's face told it all. His ship was lost and he wasn't on it. "We'll need another escort and this one may not be as cooperative."

"Guess we don't have to worry about that bad shaft bearing now, Captain. Right?" said Ears.

Chapter Seventeen

Egress

Chief Sonarman Allen Leonard had his work cut out for him. He had to get a cavitation signature from a ship inside Haiphong harbor that was dead in the water and use that unique vibration signal to guide Tunny from Haiphong—and he had to do it in a hurry.

The extra crew from the SS Jan Mayen placed an unusual burden on Tunny's berthing facilities, foodstuffs, sanitary conditions, and, most importantly, her supply of fresh air. Most of the regular crew were already "hot racking"—a practice of sleeping in unoccupied berths while the regular occupant was on watch. The additional berthing capacity in Tunny's hangar relieved most of this berthing problem, but the strain on food supplies and the capacity of the HP air tanks was crucial.

By cycling the high-pressure air through the boat while simultaneously operating the air compressors, Tunny could keep the air in her hull oxygenated. But this technique wouldn't work for long with all the extra bodies on board. Normally, Tunny could stay submerged indefinitely as long as she could snorkel and draw in fresh air with her massive diesel engines. But now she was parked on the bottom in a hostile port and it was full daylight. The CO_2 detectors were registering 'critical' only two hours after bottoming. The lithium hydroxide scrubbers were activated and the smoking lamp was extinguished to preserve oxygen. Extinguishing the smoking lamp was irrelevant—no lighter or match could be struck anyway because of the polluted air.

Browne calculated they had till noon to clear the harbor or they would have to rise to snorkel depth to keep the crew from suffocating.

Meanwhile, Ears was working hard to come up with a solution the problem. He could receive passive signals from almost every ship in the harbor. He began looking for one that was anchored out in the river. Machines on board these ships were constantly in motion to supply the ship's needs. Water pumps, diesel engines, air compressors, electric motors, and numerous other mechanical devices made noise. Ears could hear these noises and was able to catalog them by type and frequency.

All he had to do now was record the sundry noises of the more than thirty-five ships in port, catalog them by frequency and equipment type and then discover which of the ships was leaving Haiphong. Here he got lucky.

The "bombing" of the harbor caused a great deal of confusion and activity in the harbor. Ears picked up the sounds of a medium freighter lighting its boilers and making preparations for getting underway. He signaled the Conn when he heard the anchor chain rattling against the hull and spilling into the chain locker.

"Captain, I got us one! Let's get ready to move!"

No one had left their bottoming watch stations and it was now 0930 hours. Some of the crew had been on watch for more than 48 hours straight. Mike had let Jackson and Hennesey catnap, as had many of the crew in the Conning Tower. But adrenaline had kept them all awake and alert. A new sense of urgency now infected the crew and Mike called for turns on the screws and began having Woodsey pump water from the trim tanks to again attain neutral buoyancy.

Tunny came up to 59 feet and the Browne took a look around. "Where's our escort?" asked the Skipper.

"Ears says he's at 210 degrees and somewhere between 1500 and 2000 yards distant," replied the Navigator. Snuffy was working the DRT using the old French plots and Turner was double-checking. Skein translated the French markings to English. The Skipper swung the scope around to 210 degrees and focused upon the intended target. The Torpedo Data Computer (TDC) automatically calculated the Closest Point of Approach and it was fed to the DRT for inclusion in the escape route from the harbor.

Browne determined that Ears' random choice for an escort was a Chinese freighter out of Shanghai. It was a rusty old bucket with its name and hull number inscribed in Mandarin Chinese on its fantail. It was forced to make a maneuver of 180 degrees to face downriver. Its Captain completed the change of heading with practiced skill. He threw his engines into reverse, holding a static position in the river until the pilot boat could be sent from shore.

Tunny was already headed downstream and was using her screws to keep from drifting with the current. She waited for the Chinese freighter to come abeam before falling in astern.

By this time, Ears had determined a cavitation signature for the old freighter and could now determine distance to the target with his volume and frequency equipment. He directed Browne to within 100 yards of the old tub and prayed that the skimmer would maintain a constant speed. The speed of the target was now critical. Should she slow for any reason, Tunny would have to veer rapidly to avoid ramming the freighter. Any change in course could result in entering the minefields at the harbor mouth. Should the freighter increase speed for any reason, Tunny would fall behind and miss her chance to cross the submarine cable undetected.

Ears could detect a change in speed by counting the freighter's screw revolutions. These changes had to be quickly sent to maneuvering to avoid disaster for Tunny. For this reason, the IC (Interior Communications) Electricians had wired the 7MC directly into Sonar. This way the Maneuvering crew could anticipate speed changes without orders from the Conn. Seconds made a difference between death or capture and survival in this tense situation.

It was only Browne's unflinching faith in the skill of his crew that allowed him to relinquish even this small grip on the command of his ship. Bill Browne listened intently to the conversation between Sonar and Maneuvering. "God," he prayed, "these guys are just kids! The lives of all these people under my command are in the hands of kids!"

Simon stood at the helm wearing a sound powered phone headset. Ears gave him course changes directly and he responded as if the orders were coming directly from the Conning Officer. He had mastered the one-degree correction in Tunny's helm. His brain automatically subtracted one degree from every course command to keep the bent old boat on the correct heading.

It took two hours to navigate through the minefield and across the submarine nets. Ears heard the chain descend to allow the freighter access to open water; he had maneuvered to close the distance to Tunny's unsuspecting escort. Tunny cleared the chain at 1145 hours local time. She surfaced 1000 yards aft of the Chinese tub and threw a scare into her crew.

Snuffy Smith was the first to crack the conning tower hatch. The rush of fresh air caused momentary rapture. He fell to the deck unconscious.

Captain Browne set a speed course to Subic. He broke radio silence with SubFlot Seven to announce the failure of his mission.

Chapter Eighteen

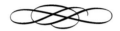

A Letter from Home

"Dear Burris,

I have good news and even better news! Daddy is fine after his sudden spell. The doctors say it was an angina attack and should be a warning to him to take better care of himself.

He went back to work yesterday on a different schedule that allows him to reduce his activity. I think the attack scared him enough to make him change his lifestyle. He quit smoking and he even eats a salad once in awhile. He looks much better and he seems to have more energy than he's had in years.

Now for the "even better" news. I'm coming to Manila!

That's right—to the Philippine Islands—to Manila! I got a job with the Peace Corps teaching English to Spanish-speaking people. They say that a lot of folks in Manila speak Spanish and they need a translator and teacher there. My three years of Spanish helped me pass the test and when I told them I wanted to take the job in Manila, they couldn't wait to get me there. I guess it isn't one of the 'garden spots' for the Peace Corps.

I should be in Manila by the time you get this letter as I leave on July the 19th. Daddy is really worried about me, but I am so excited I'm about to pee my pants! Can you get away for a few days to visit? The address is..."

Tim got mad! What the hell did this silly little child think she was doing! He hadn't heard from his Dad about the "attack," which didn't surprise him. Fred Lang, characteristically, wouldn't want to worry him. So why didn't Alice stay in Houston to make sure he was taking care of himself? Instead, she was rampaging all over the world with the stupid Peace Corps! He'd see about this!

He consulted the pin-up girl calendar on the hangar bulkhead. Today was July 30th. Alice could have been in the PI for over a week by now. Hell, she might already be dead! He immediately took Alice's letter to Chief Keller and asked for a pass to Manila.

"No one is allowed to travel to Manila alone. We always use the 'buddy system' for that trip. Too many Huks along the way for a lone sailor," said Keller.

"How 'bout if David and Simon come with me, Chief? Okay then?"

"Oh, all right. But just for four days—no more. I need your sorry asses here to get the Old Girl back to sea where she belongs."

Tim never heard the part about getting Tunny back to sea—in mid sentence he had headed aft at flank speed to find his friends.

Chapter Ninteen

Voodoo

Jim Woods and Eddie Rance had been working on the prank for several weeks. They had been having trouble with the logistics, however. They finally decided they needed a third accomplice. It had to be someone that was in their duty section so they all three could be on liberty at the same time. They tossed the idea about between themselves for a couple of days and finally landed on the perfect suspect.

Jim approached Roger one day while they were on watch. He explained the whole setup and asked Roger to man the "lookout" station. Roger readily agreed.

Three days after they returned from Yankee Station off Haiphong, the three conspirators began to hatch their plot. They picked Pauline's Bar, across the street from the Home Port at the corner of Rizal and Magsaysay, to commit the offense.

It was about 1700 when Woodsey entered Pauline's and sat at the bar. The bar was just inside the front door on a raised platform above the dance floor. Pauline's was huge for an Olongapo gin joint—probably around 2,000 square feet and at least two stories high. There was an overlooking balcony that was perched on three sides of the dance floor. The raised platform that accommodated the bar also surrounded the dance floor and was big enough to hold tables and chairs. The balcony and raised platform were protected by a hand rail on turned posts that was table height. On the dance floor level, two steps down from the bar, were several other tables and chairs just off the polished oak floor. Opposite the bar was the stage where the "dancers" performed. It was too far early for any performers on this particular day.

Jim quickly ordered a double shot of Old Charter and slapped 50 pesos on the lacquered bar top. The familiar sound of money hitting the bar instantly drew a crowd of Pauline's hostesses. Jim's hand shook violently as he raised the shot glass to his lips. He threw the whiskey down in one gulp and ordered another shot immediately. His hands shook and he looked nervously around the room, as if searching for someone he knew.

A particularly shapely hostess finally got Jim's attention. "What you so shaky for sailor? Just relax. Buy me a drink."

"What's your name?" asked Jim.

"Margaret my name—what's yours?"

"Jim—call me Jim. Bartender!" yelled Woodsey, "Give Margaret a champagne cocktail!" Margaret was ecstatic! Champagne cocktails contained nothing but 7-Up, maraschino cherry juice, and ice. She got half the cost of the drink without any of the complications of an alcohol hang over. She decided to latch on to this sucker for the entire night.

Just then Eddie entered through the front door. He waited inside for a minute until his eyes adjusted to the dim light. Then he began searching around the room with a menacing countenance on his face. His glance landed on Jim and he mouthed several colorful phrases under his breath. If looks could kill, Woodsey would have been dead instantly.

Eddie then moved to a table on the dance floor and summoned a hostess. He ordered a bourbon and soda and told his hostess to buy herself a champagne cocktail. Opal, Eddie's unsuspecting hostess, mimicked Margaret's glee. She had found a real prize for the evening, even if he was a little morose. Eddie continued to stare daggers at Jim.

Roger sauntered into Pauline's about this time and strolled across the dance floor to a table on the raised platform on the opposite side of the room from Eddie. He was in full view of both conspirators. Neither Jim nor Eddie appeared to notice the new arrival. Roger ordered a Sam Miguel and ignored any attempt by a hostess to join him at his table.

Jim's face had flushed red with the arrival of Eddie and his hands began to shake even more violently. He turned away from Eddie and ordered his third shot of whiskey. His voice began to quiver as he ordered Margaret another champagne cocktail.

"Sailor," exclaimed Margaret, "What's a matta you? You sick or somethin'?"

Jim barely got the third shot to his lips as his hands were shaking so much. He splashed some of the drink on his shirt front. He began to talk to Margaret.

Eddie continued his icy glare at Jim. Opal couldn't help but notice his visible animosity toward what she did not know. "Hey, sailor, why you so mad? I do somethin' to piss you off?"

"It ain't you, Baby," said Eddie, "It's that scum of humanity sitting at the bar over there!" Eddie gestured toward Jim. Jim was the only sailor at the bar.

"Is that guy behind me on the dance floor still staring at me?" asked Jim.

"Yeah," said Margaret, "He look like he want to kill you!"

Jim let out a slight moan and swallowed the whiskey in one gulp. "Barkeep! Another shot for me and another cocktail for the lady." Margaret knew she wouldn't have to work for a week after she was done rolling this sucker. She leaned a sympathetic head on his shoulder. "Talk to Margaret and tell me what's a matta!"

"Talk to Opal, sailor. Tell me why you soooo mad!" Olongapo bar hogs must have heard every sob story in the world after they had worked the bars for a couple of years. Margaret and Opal were old hands at listening to drunken sailors bemoan their pitiful existence. The more they displayed mock sympathy, the more champagne cocktails they sold, and the more pesos came their way.

"About ten years ago that asshole at the bar and I were best friends," said Eddie.

"About ten years ago that creep at that table behind me was my best friends," said Jim.

"I was a priest and he was a merchant seaman. We had grown up together on the same block in Brooklyn," explained Eddie.

"I was a merchant seamen and he was a priest. We grew up on the same street in New York," said Jim. "He had a little sister who wanted to join the church to be a nun. I was in love with her and she dumped me for the god-damned church!" exclaimed Jim harshly.

"He always loved my little sister. But she wanted to be a nun and help people," said Eddie. "But that bastard couldn't stand losing her to the church.

"One day his ship docked in New York and he came by to see me at the church school. My sister worked there, too, as a teacher. We three old friends started talking and after work continued talking at the local pub." Eddie's voice grew more vitriolic with every word that passed his lips.

Jim was explaining the same sequence of events to Margaret. "We ended up in a local bar and were having a great time talking over old times in high school and in the neighborhood. Father Eddie—that's the guy staring at me—got a call from the church and had to leave suddenly. His sister and I kept talking and I kept drinking and one thing led to another till I almost passed out. Mary, Father Eddie's little sister, called a cab and took me back to my hotel room to sleep it off. I guess I wasn't as drunk as she thought, 'cause I grabbed her and raped her when she took me to my room."

Eddie's story was much the same. "That SOB took advantage of my sister, the novice nun, when she was just doing him a kindly act by taking him back to his room. She had to quit the church and what she always wanted to be. Right then I renounced my vows and swore that if ever I caught up to that motherfucker, I'd kill him on sight!"

Jim explained to Margaret, "After he found out what I did to his sister, he swore he'd kill me on sight. I've been running from him for the last ten years. He finally caught up to me today here in Olongapo. That's him sittin' at that table over there lookin' like he could kill right here. You gotta keep me here until he leaves or he'll kill me for sure!" pleaded Jim. He began to sob and whimper. Margaret moved closer and put her arm around his shaking shoulders. She slid her hand down his back to feel for his wallet.

Eddie mysteriously produced a wrinkled brown paper bag from under the table. No one had noticed it when he walked in. "Do you know voodoo?" he asked Opal.

"Yes, black magic," said Opal. A puzzled look spread over her face as she watched Eddie pull what appeared to be a small likeness of Jim from the paper bag.

"In my travels over the last ten years, I used my training as a priest and combined it with the teachings of voodoo. I am a voodoo master now. Do you know what this voodoo doll means?"

"Oh, yes," said Opal. Voodoo was well known in the Philippines, brought there by Spanish slave traders and their human cargo from the East Coast of Africa. Many native Filipinos still practiced voodoo out of sight of the Catholic Church. Opal knew exactly what the voodoo doll represented. She could not mistake the doll's likeness to the miserable sailor seated at the bar with her friend, Margaret.

Jim's head was buried in Margaret's bosom, but he still kept an eye on Roger across the dance floor.

Eddie then produced a switchblade knife recently purchased at a local curio shop. Opal's eyes widened as Eddie flipped the blade open with a snap. He laid the doll on the table. It's hair was the same color as Jim's and, with the exception of the shoes, wore the same shirt and pants that adorned Jim's shaking body. In the dim light of Pauline's, the doll looked exactly like Jim Woods.

"Today is the day I exact my revenge for my poor sister!" exclaimed Eddie. He raised his hand well above his head. The dagger was clutched in a stabbing position as Eddie's eyes widened and his voice became shrill.

Roger quickly ran his hand through his hair. Jim caught the gesture and listened sharply for the sound of the knife hitting the ketchup-engorged baby doll.

Eddie proclaimed in a voice loud enough to be heard everywhere in Pauline's, "Today he dies for his sin!" Eddie drove the knife into the baby doll. The force of the dagger thrust forced the ketchup through the puncture, squirting the red fluid into the air and all over everything and anybody nearby. Opal's dress was covered in the tomato extract.

Simultaneously, Jim slapped the ketchup-engorged prophylactic in his left shirt pocket. The blood red tomato substance oozed through his fingers and the red stain spread across his chest. Jim shouted, "He's killed me!" He dramatically staggered to his feet, walked to the railing that separated the bar from the dance floor, and toppled over the rail. He landed athletically on a table that collapsed under his weight.

Opal yelled hysterically, "He killed him! He killed him!" She ran into the street covered in ketchup, terrifying everyone in sight.

Margaret screamed and fainted.

Eddie squeezed the last of the ketchup from the doll and left Pauline's for the Home Port at a run.

At this point, their little prank began to come apart. Roger was supposed to act like a hospital corpsman and escort Jim to the door for medical attention. However, a crowd began to gather around Woodsey as he lay in mock agony on the dance floor. Roger could not get to Jim because an assemblage of hostesses, bar tenders and innocent Pauline's patrons had gathered to witness his demise. Roger then heard the first of several sirens as they began to head toward the disturbance in Pauline's. He discreetly ducked out a side door and headed to Home Port in Eddie's wake.

This left poor Jim, soaked in tomato ketchup, lying on the floor of Pauline's surrounded by shocked bystanders. The crowd was calling for the police, the Shore Patrol, a doctor—anybody that could help this "victim" of black magic.

Jim made a quick command decision. He began to groan in mock agony as he staggered to his feet. "I'm OK!" he repeated over and over. "I'm OK!" He wobbled to the front door, shoving people aside, holding his "wounded" chest and moaning in mock pain. He ran head on into two Shore Patrolmen.

They escorted him to the drunk wagon while his erstwhile friends regaled the patrons at the Home Port with their tale of derring-do.

Chapter Twenty

AWOL

Roger was alone and slowly came to the realization that he was awake. He only became aware that he was no longer slept because of the constant aching throb in his forehead right between his eyes. He had no memory of where he was or how he got there. The more he regained consciousness, the stronger the throb in his head.

He was lying on his left side with his left eye buried in a pillow. He slowly opened his right eye. The bright light of day entered his pupil and accentuated his headache. He swiftly slammed his eye shut. The pain eased somewhat.

He then rocked his head slightly so as to open his left eye. His nose and the angle of the light from the window shaded his left eye so it was not as painful to open. He began to move his head from side to side slowly. He did not recognize his surroundings. He was lying on a straw mat no more than three inches off the floor. There were few furnishings in the room—a chair and a small table that held a basin and pitcher. The door was covered with a lavender-colored curtain and there was one window about six feet from the foot of his bed. His was not covered with anything and the only clothing he felt on his body was his socks, his GI underwear, and his dog tags. He was sweating profusely.

He heard street sounds from outside the window that stood open. He smelled the now familiar aromas of Olongapo—sewage, rotten vegetation and barbecued monkey meat.

He remembered Tunny's victorious return after her Haiphong mission. After the prank at Pauline's, he and Eddie had joined liberty crew that had retired to the Home Port. White Russians were the special drink of the day—2 pesos apiece. "White Russians"—how apropos, they'd thought.

Most of the crew got drunk and headed for the barracks to sleep it off. But Roger had felt more adventurous. He decided to stay for awhile longer at the Home Port Lounge. The last memory he had was staggering into Jane's arms in a booth at his favorite watering hole.

"That must be where I am," he thought, "in the whorehouse next to the Home Port!" But he had been there several times before and this room was not familiar. He pushed himself to a sitting position with great effort. His head felt like it was about to explode! He struggled to his feet and looked around for the rest of his wardrobe.

Nothing! No uniform, no shoes, no white hat, no watch, no ring, no wallet—nothing!

He rubbed his temples to relieve some of the pain and started toward the door of the room. He stumbled and caught himself by the curtain door. It tore from its anchors and crumbled to the floor with him. Using the wall to steady his progress, Roger once more climbed to his feet. He was a little more steady now and the increased blood circulation began to make his aching head feel better.

He looked out the door to discover a hallway he had never seen before—or at least he could not remember seeing before. He was definitely not in the Home Port Hotel. He saw a wooden door down the hall to his left and set a course to investigate. He worked the latch, opened the door and found the common toilet.

He moved to the urinal and took the longest piss he could remember in his short life. He then puked into the toilet. The smell of his vomit caused him to regurgitate again and again until he was left kneeling over the bowl dry heaving. It took what seemed like an hour for the nausea to leave him. He then left the benjo (Japanese for toilet) and began to search for his clothes. He found a stairway at the opposite end of the hall from the benjo and descended to the first floor.

It was a hotel all right, but one he had never visited previously. He went to the make-shift front desk—a plank laying across several saw horses—and banged on the bell for service. The ringing bell sent pulses of renewed pain through his skull.

After several minutes of waiting for no one to appear, Roger moved around the desk and into a small office just off the "lobby."

He shouted, "Anyone home?"

There was no reply so he began to search through the several boxes and crates stacked about the small room. What he discovered made his blood run cold.

There were several hundred US Military ID cards, thousands of watches, rings and other assorted jewelry items, military uniforms from all services and thousands of dollars in US currency and military pay script (MPCs). He even found several Shore Patrol armbands, nightsticks, and sidearms. He then made the chilling discovery of his own wallet with his ID still inside. Roger realized that they planned to kill him. Whatever had happened to delay them in their task was pure serendipity on Roger's behalf.

He dug into the boxes of uniforms and found his sizes in trousers, shirt, and shoes. Once clothed, he looked through the jewelry box for his watch and class ring. He found only his watch—it read 1030 hours. He was AWOL—absent without leave!

He panicked and moved swiftly toward the door of the small office. He ran right into the hotel proprietor, knocking him backwards into the lobby. The reception desk crashed to the floor and the hostler began a tirade of Tagalong obscenities at the top of his voice. Roger grabbed him by the shirt front and threw him into the street—while he still yelled for help.

Now Roger got mad! He lost control and he slugged the little Filipino desk clerk twice in the mouth. Blood spurted from split lips and broken teeth. The little man pulled himself upright and ran to Roger's right, down Rizal, screaming at the top of his lungs for help.

Roger began to look around to get his bearings. He calmed somewhat when he saw Pauline's and the Home Port, at the intersection of Rizal and Magsaysay, about 100 yards off to his left. He set a course for familiar territory and safety. His head still ached, although not as intensely now. His hands began to shake from fright and alcohol withdrawals.

It was too early for Pauline to open her bar, but the drug store next door was open for local traffic. He went in and asked for some aspirin. When he realized he had not taken any of the cash from the whorehouse, he went back outside and headed down Magsaysay for the Base. He got about a half a mile before the Shore Patrol picked him up and took him to the Brig.

The next day the Old Man heard his story at Captains' Mast. The little "hotel" was raided within an hour and the proprietor was arrested and imprisoned.

Roger was found to have taken an unauthorized liberty while behind on his qualifications. In addition, he had been AWOL and out of uniform. He was given 10 days in the Brig and fined $200.

Chapter Twenty-One

Alice Lang

"Gee whiz," she said to the stewardess as she left the plane, "it sure is hot here!"

Alice's shoulder-length blond hair quickly went limp in the humid tropical climate. Perspiration broke out on her face and her make-up immediately began to run. But she remained beautiful. She drew every eye as she walked from the recently arrived jet across the tarmac toward Manila's International Airport. She was just under 5' 7" tall with classic long legs and a perfectly proportioned figure. Her angelic face couldn't mask her smile of excitement.

The Peace Corp ambassador grudgingly sent to the Airport to retrieve their latest recruit had a sudden change of heart when Alice recognized the cardboard sign he held. It read:

Peace Corps
Alice Lang

in bold hand-written letters.

"Good God," he thought to himself, "no one that pretty joins the Peace Corps." He had been accustomed to the austere Vassar-types with their unmanaged hippie haircuts, unshaven legs and weathered New England complexions. The Peace Corps during the 60's was a refuge for the anti-war crowd as long as service therein kept them from the war zone. The pseudo-sophisticated college pro-testors joined in blind flocks to answer John Kennedy's call so they could visit exotic ports-of-call at government expense.

But this woman was different, the young ambassador decided. Besides her obvious beauty, there was a happy air about her that would disarm even the most cynical of their membership. The way she carried her head high and the eagerness in her blue eyes announced her sincerity and signaled her purity of spirit. To the uninformed, she appeared to be naive. But under that deceptive exterior appearance beat a heart of strength and resiliency that had been tempered by experience beyond her years. One imagined a depth to her soul that could not be reached through casual contact.

"That's me," shouted Alice. She was wearing blue jeans that fit her form closely. Her Foley's blouse was more of a western-style red and white checkered shirt tucked at her slim waist. Her high-heeled ladies Lacona boots looked out of place in these oriental surroundings. She carried only a small bag and had a raincoat draped over her arm. With the monsoon season at hand the raincoat would have appeared to be standard apparel. However, the heat and humidity at this latitude made any kind of outer garment superfluous. An umbrella was much more practical, assuming one could keep its shape in the monsoon winds.

"I'm Alice Lang!" she yelled across the tarmac.

The Peace Corps ambassador lowered the sign and extended his had in greeting as she approached. "Bob Wilson, Alice. And I must say, you look smashing!" Bob was from Long Island and had purposely cultivated Harvard-ese into his speech. She took his extended hand and was met with a cold limp-fish grip.

"Burris would call this guy a pussy!" she thought. "Thanks, Bob," she said aloud. "Where do we go to get my luggage?"

"Just you don't worry your pretty little head about your baggage, Alice," he said in a condescending manner. "I'll have Jesus here, our local liaison officer, deal with that problem. Have you your claim tickets?" Jesus was a small dark-skinned oriental gentleman of middle age. He had been standing unobtrusively next to Bob all this time.

Alice reached into her bag and produced the required documents. "You're probably too big a swish to handle luggage, Bob", she thought. Jesus took the claim checks and headed out with a purpose.

"How nice of Jesus," Alice said aloud. "Which way to the cab?"

"This way, Alice. And down here we call them Jitneys. They are well suited for the road and climatic conditions encountered in this God-forsaken place.

"You will soon learn," he continued, "how very primitive the living conditions are here. Why, these heathens even harbor pet lizards to reduce the cockroach population in their homes. Homes, indeed!" he continued with obvious contempt, "Mostly wooden ramshackle huts with corrugated tin roofs. They eat in one corner, sleep in another, maintain their chickens in the third and defecate, pardon my language, in the fourth. It is only during the monsoons that these shelters are cleansed, if then."

Bob's disgust with the locals was more than obvious. His air of superiority turned Alice against him immediately. Her experiences in Houston with the indigent and underprivileged provided her with a sense of tolerance and an admiration for people who overcame hardship and deprivation. Bob and his pampered friends could never understand their plight or their quiet dignity. She wasn't sure these effete Eastern-types understood the Peace Corps goals.

They were propelled through the Manila streets at an almost breakneck speed. Jesus had provided the jitney driver directions in Tagalong. Alice noticed the similarity in the accents of the native Filipinos and that of the Spanish-speaking inhabitants of the Southwestern US. Even some of the Tagalong words were of Spanish origin. No wonder a Spanish teacher was needed here, she thought.

They arrived within 30 minutes at a non-descript concrete block building across the street from the US Embassy. The Peace Corps headquarters was in the middle of a governmental complex. Several foreign embassies and Philippine government buildings were clustered within easy walking distance of each other. The staff inside the building was anxious to greet their new colleague and Bob Wilson happily guided Alice through the maze of offices and introductions with his now characteristic snotty aplomb.

Two hours later, an exhausted Alice was finally escorted to the Peace Corps dormitory. She shared a large room with about ten other female college-age volunteers. The community bath was at the end of a long hall that passed by the boys dorm room. Alice made her first trip to the showers to a chorus of wolf whistles and cat-calls. Her embarrassment was well concealed and she took the hazing as if it was well intended—which it was.

After a long shower and a supper of insipid vegetables and stringy chipped beef on toast, she climbed exhausted into an upper bunk bed that had her name stenciled at the foot.

Before she fell into a deep slumber, she thought of her adopted brother. He was close, she could feel it. Her hero was less than 100 miles away. She longed to see him, put her arms around his neck and feel his embrace at last. "I love you," she murmured just as she fell asleep.

Chapter Twenty-Two

Manila

Tim, David, and Simon arrived at the Manila bus station after a bus ride of less than 100 miles that had taken a full eight hours. The bus had stopped several times to clear checkpoints established by local authorities in vain attempts to quell the Huk rebellion.

The Huks were communist guerillas in constant conflict with the Marcos regime. Sometimes these uprisings cost lives on both sides and often these lives were of innocent bystanders. The US Navy sanctioned the bus trip to Manila only if it could be accomplished during daylight hours. No sailor or soldier was allowed to travel alone and no bus was allowed out of Olongapo without a police escort to the next constabulary's district. Despite these precautions, two Enterprise sailors had disappeared within the last six months and were as yet missing.

During the ride, they discussed Roger's Article 32 punishment. Tim told David and Simon of the episode on the Jan Mayen and of his suspicions of Roger.

"I don't know guys, but I'm not sure anybody can count on him for nothin'. He's kind of a Momma's Boy, anyway. I seen 'em before. They's always afraid!"

David listened, but still felt sorry for Roger. Maybe the AWOL episode would wake Roger up. Maybe he would respond to the punishment positively. David hoped so, anyway. One thing for sure, they wouldn't get drunk in the Home Port from then on.

The three sailors had been wearing tropical whites when they left Olongapo. But by now they had changed to civilian clothes to draw less attention to themselves. That they were US military was unmistakable, however. The way they walked in march step and their military haircuts were a dead give away.

The cramped seating and the close atmosphere of the bus had taken their toll on the Tunny sailors. Each walked stiffly and stooped over to the bus door, thankful to feel the circulation return to their legs and feet.

Alice was waiting for them. She ran toward Tim as he staggered off the bus.

"Burris! Burris!" she shouted and waved over the crowd. She almost tackled him to the ground as she threw herself into his arms.

He put his arms around her and hugged back as he struggled to maintain his balance and keep from falling.

"Alice," was his only reply. He loved his little sister and was genuinely happy to see her. He held her for a full two minutes repeating her name over and over again. He missed her more than he had realized. The memory of her splattered with Katy's blood returned to him and his eyes filled with tears. "My fault," he whispered, "My fault."

"My God, you have grown, child!" He pushed her back and gave her a full body once over. He was shocked at how much she had filled out over the last year and a half. He was proud of her and mad at her simultaneously.

"Why are you here? What's come over you to come to this place? And with the goddam Peace Corps at that? Don't ya know they're nothin' but a bunch of college drop-out jerk offs dodgin' the draft?"

She extended her lower lip in mock angst. She knew he was glad to see her and she was flattered by his worry. The false frown quickly melted into a full grin as he hugged her once more and kissed her cheek.

David was astounded. This woman was an unexpected vision. He had agreed to come with Tim only because Tim had pleaded and he wanted to help him with a family problem. David hadn't expected to be greeted with such female beauty. He had expected Tim's little sister to be a short pimply faced version of the Burris he had known over the last few months since sub school. Alice was more than a pleasant surprise.

He caught her glance and nodded. She smiled at him and tapped Tim on the shoulder, "Aren't you gonna introduce your friends, silly boy?"

Tim turned to face his two shipmates. He had forgotten his manners momentarily and he was embarrassed.

"Yeah, sure," he said, "This is David Jackson. He's been my runnin' mate ever since sub school. And this here Hebrew is Simon Berg, the best damned helmsman in the whole damn Navy. Fellas, this here snot-nosed kid is my little sister, Alice."

Alice extended her hand, "I feel like I already know you both. Burris has written so much about you." Her handshake was firm. David thought he could feel her pulse when they gripped. Or was that his heart beating?

"Must have been awfully boring reading if that is all Tim had to write about. Nice to finally meet you Alice. Tim has spoken of you often, but he never told me you were so beautiful." David held her hand a little longer than she expected. She didn't seem to mind as he looked into her eyes. Before she pulled her hand away, David was in love.

"Nice to meet you too, David," she blushed slightly.

Alice reached for Simon's hand as well, but was surprised to see him staring wide-eyed at the young lady standing next to her. It was now Alice's turn to be embarrassed.

"I'm so sorry," she said. "This is Miss Drusilla Gomez, our liaison officer at Peace Corps. She has been nice enough to show me around and was kind enough to come with me to the bus station. She is also teaching me to understand Tagalog.

"Drusilla, this is my Brother, Burris Lang and his shipmates David Jackson and Simon Berg. They have come to Manila to scold me for joining the Peace Corps."

Everyone laughed at Alice's self-effacement except Simon. His gaze was still firmly stuck on Drusilla.

Drusilla was Eurasian; her mother was from Filipino aristocracy and her father was a Spanish merchant whose family had settled in the Philippines prior to the American colonization. She was about 5'4" tall, had perfect black hair that reached well down her back and she had the bluest eyes under the tropical sun. Simon could not take his eyes from her face and his voice was silent for the first time in his life. He was captivated by her oriental beauty. So he simply extended his hand toward her, eyes wide open.

Finally, he found his voice, "Hello," was all he could manage.

In perfect Oxford English came Drusilla's reply, "Hello, friends of Alice. Welcome to my city."

Simon gently took the extended hand and brought it to his lips in mock medieval chivalry. "This is the best welcome I've had since...ever!" Simon faltered.

They all had a quick laugh that broke the ice, shook hands, and hugged all around.

"Say," said Alice, "who's this Tim guy you are talking about? I don't know any Tim!"

"That's me, Alice. Nobody likes the name 'Burris' so Chief Keller and me decided to use Tim from now on. You can call me Tim, too! All my close friends do!"

"Well, I guess then Tim it is...since I want to remain one of your 'close' friends."

Alice wanted there to be so much more between them. She had loved him all her life and he was her hero—her knight in shining armor—her Galahad. But she saw it in his eyes now as it had always been for Burris.

For Tim, she was his sister and a sibling. Burris—Tim—could feel nothing more. Tim knew Ans' death would always be between them. That and the image of her standing in the hall, splattered with Katy's blood and terrified by the carnage that had happened before her young eyes. Tim would never forgive himself for letting that happen. He knew what Ans had been capable of doing. He could have stopped it had he only had the courage. Tim couldn't look at Alice without feeling guilty.

The five young people loaded luggage into a Toyota jitney and headed for the Peace Corps building. The boys' dorm had several extra bunks and they had agreed to put Tim and his friends up for a few nights while they toured Manila.

They dumped the bags in the dorm and headed out to see the sights. After a couple of hours of hiking around in the tropical heat, the sun was obscured by monsoon rain clouds and the sky fell in.

During the monsoon season, it rained almost constantly. Sometimes it would let up a little and seem to rest at a drizzle for a while, then it would rain again. Commonly, rainfall amounts would exceed 10" a day and the primitive drainage systems would begin to fail.

David and Alice found themselves sitting under an awning at one of the many al fresco restaurants in the city. Somehow, Drusilla had convinced Tim and Simon to accompany her to a museum across the avenue. "Willing dupes," thought David. He had feigned exhaustion and convinced Alice (with the promise of a frozen daiquiri) to stay with him at the pub while the others ventured on.

"Alice," spoke David, "what did Tim mean when he said it was his fault at the bus station?"

David was just trying to make conversation, but he was shocked when Alice's face clouded over like the monsoon day they were now experiencing.

"I'm sorry," he said. "I didn't mean to bring up unpleasant memories." He looked her in the eyes as they began to fill with tears.

"No," said Alice. "I should be the one to say 'I'm sorry' for spoiling such a fun day. How much has Bur...I mean Tim told you about his family?"

"Oh, not a lot. I knew about you and your Dad and that you lived in Texas—Houston, I think. He really admires your Dad and he thinks the world of you. He doesn't talk much about anything else. Simon and I really learned most of what we know on the bus ride here from Subic. I guess we just never thought much about Tim's life before we met at Sub School."

Over the next thirty minutes, Alice deliberately related her remembrances of the night Katy Lang was murdered. "...and Bur... I mean Tim hasn't been the same since Daddy killed Ansel. He seems to think there was something else he could have done to save Katy's life, I think. He just carries the blame of it around with him like a big 'toe sack on his back. Sometimes I could even see him bend his shoulders to the load, it seemed.

"But now he seems really changed. It's like that load has gone away. He walks straighter and he seems more comfortable and he is the Burris I remember before that night Katy died. Do you think the new name is the reason for the change, David?"

"Alice, I don't think it's just the name change," said David. "I don't remember him any other way than the way he is now. But when Chief Keller began to call him Tim, he seemed to really like it. Keller put him in charge of our detail and he did a great job those first few days. Tim is a good guy—my friend—and Simon and I and

Tim are 'mates. That's how it is in the Boats—Submarine Service—guys build close friendships, like brothers almost. Our lives depend on one another. We help each other 'cause we know that the other guy would do the same for us.

"It's hard to explain, Alice, unless you've been there. But I know without lookin' that Tim will do what he is supposed to do. And he knows he can rely on Simon and me and all the other guys on Tunny to do what we're supposed to do. That's the way it is on Tunny from the Old Man right down to the mess cook—we each do our jobs—and we all help each other with everything else. No one gives up, no one quits because he knows everyone else is countin' on him.

"Tim is part of that and it makes him a better guy for it. It makes us all better guys. Maybe that's what you are seeing that is different now with Tim." He paused and looked across the table at Alice.

She was smiling. The smile made her even more beautiful and David was suddenly embarrassed. "I guess I've just rambled on and bored you to laughter. I hope I didn't make a fool of myself."

"No, David," said Alice. "You did not make a fool of yourself! Quite the opposite—maybe I'll never know how much you men devote yourselves to Tunny, but she has made me very jealous. I only wish Tim could feel about me the way he feels about that submarine."

David saw it in her eyes as they began to fill with tears again. Her love for Tim was beyond that of just a sister. "How long have you been in love with Tim?"

"Since I first laid eyes on him after Daddy and Mother got married. Me and Katy and Burris were close—almost as close as you guys. We did the housework, helped each other with chores and homework and looked to each other for help when there was a fight to be fought.

"Ansel was always an outsider. He was too busy making trouble to be part of the family. He was selfish, David. Maybe he deserved to die, but his and Katy's death changed Burris and for that I'll never forgive him. I think he killed Katy on impulse, 'cause he was scared. But fighting Daddy for the gun was on purpose and so Daddy had to shoot him. Burris saw all that and it made him different, somehow. Like I said, he always seemed to be carrying a hundred pound sack full of potatoes around on his back after that."

David withdrew his GI handkerchief from his back pocket and handed it to Alice to wipe her tears. "I'm so sorry I asked, Alice. I didn't mean to spoil your reunion with Tim. I hope you'll forgive me for bringing it up."

"David, I should be asking you to forgive me. I'm so silly sometimes over this, but you are the first person I feel like I can talk to. You, Simon and Burris are such good friends that I finally felt like I could talk to someone. I shouldn't have burdened you with our problems. Ya'll have enough to deal with on that old submarine."

David caught sight of the three museum visitors as they crossed the street to join them at the restaurant. Simon, Drusilla, and Tim were talking and laughing as if there wasn't a war going on. And for this day only, there wasn't.

Chapter Twenty-Three

Sea Trials

The next three days were a whirlwind tour of the oriental city of Manila during the monsoon season. There were parts of Manila that were contemporary and included modern conveniences like indoor plumbing and even electricity part of the day. However, most of the city was squalid and many of the inhabitants lived in abject poverty. These residents worked at menial jobs in the many clothing factories in Manila. Their annual salaries were usually less than a Tunny sailor made in a month—before sub pay.

Alice and Drusilla marched the unsuspecting American sailors around town at a heated pace, dodging monsoon rainstorms along the way. The guys had almost a month's pay in their ass pockets and that made them rich by Filipino standards. They ate well; they drank fine wine and San Miguel beer, they went to the Manila symphony, and Simon fell in love.

He knew his parents would never approve. Drusilla was a gentile and an oriental one at that. For Simon to even consider a long-term commitment to Drusilla would crush his family. To marry outside the faith was an unforgivable sin; but to marry outside their race was to condemn him to everlasting Hades.

Simon knew all this. But he could not stop himself. Drusilla was all that he ever dreamed about. She was brilliant, athletically active, inquisitive, and painfully beautiful. Their conversations included their tastes in classical music, their shared theories on cuisine, their mutual interest in Middle Eastern history, and their mutual ambitions to have a family.

When it was time to board the bus back to Subic, Simon had

already made a subconscious commitment to Drusilla. They exchanged addresses and Simon got her phone numbers at the Peace Corps office and at her home. He began writing her his first letter on the return bus ride. He purchased a Philippine stamp in Olongapo and mailed the missive on the spot.

David, on the other hand, sensed that his affection for Alice would remain only platonic as long as she was devoted to Tim. The tragedy of this unrequited love was not lost on David, while Tim was completely unaware of Alice's true feelings. David thought often that he may as well tell Tim how Alice felt. But he knew the telling would offend Tim and, perhaps, even affect their friendship; that David couldn't abide.

Roger greeted them on their return to Tunny. He seemed to look better than he had in weeks. The restricted duty had dried Roger out, so it seemed, and he was almost jovial at their arrival. He was full of questions and he seemed genuinely interested in their voyage to Manila.

Tim answered with reservations. He was curious as to why Roger was so interested in their visit to his sister. David gave a completely lackluster account of their visit—one straight from a guidebook. However, Simon was very animated about his journey. He and Roger talked in the After Battery mess about Manila and Drusilla—Drusilla and Manila. After a couple of hours of Simon's diatribe, even Roger got bored and went to his rack in the hangar.

The next day at quarters they got the word. That evening they were scheduled to leave Subic for extended "sea trials." That meant 'Nam—and for quite a while. Everyone was given two hours shore leave (in rotating shifts) to buy toiletries, cigarettes, and other expendables. They picked up their clean clothes at the barracks and dropped off those that could not be worn during extended sea duty for repair and cleaning. Some went to the Base Exchange (PX) to purchase additional dungarees.

Simon went to the pay phone outside the PX and began feeding coins into the machine as rapidly as his hands would allow. He finally got hold of Drusilla at the Peace Corps office.

"Drusilla? Is that you?" The connection was poor at best and Simon could barely hear over all the static.

"Yes, this is Drusilla Gomez. Is that you, my darling Simon?"

"Yes, Dru, it is me!" said Simon. The 'my Darling...' salutation from Drusilla made his heart race. "I'm calling to let you know not to worry if you don't hear from me for the next few weeks. Tunny is going on sea trials and we'll be at sea for a while. I will write every day, but I won't be able to mail them because of where we'll be. I just want you to know that I'll be thinking of you all the time and that I'll be in Manila as soon as I return. And one more thing—I love you."

He couldn't believe his own ears. He had just committed a cardinal sin by confessing affection to a gentile. But he didn't care. He did love her and no ancient religious dogma could change that.

Let them keep their outmoded beliefs and their inflexible rules. His life really began when he met Drusilla and he wasn't going to give her up because the God of Abraham was unforgiving. Besides, hadn't even Abraham slept with a gentile to conceive a son? If it was good enough for Abraham, it was good enough for him.

"I know you will, dear. And I'll miss you. Please take care of yourself and return to me swiftly! I'll tell Alice not to worry also."

"Please deposit another five pesos or your call will be terminated." interrupted the operator.

"I'm out of change. I'll call you as soon as we're back in port. Take care and...." The line went dead.

Simon's heart was racing. It was obvious to Simon that Drusilla cared about him! And what a gracious person to think of Alice at this time. Yes, he thought, Alice would want to know why Tim could not contact her, as well. So, his call had served two purposes; one to confess his love to Drusilla and the second to let Alice know that Tim would be out of touch, too.

Simon hurried into the PX to purchase more stationery.

Tim, David, and Roger were in the PX buying toiletries and other expendables for what they knew would be an extended voyage. David had a long list of items from Chief Vincent and Mike O'Rourke. They would not be able to get to the PX because of their duties aboard ship.

Mike had to supervise the process of taking on stores and ammunition. One of the COB's several duties, as senior enlisted man, was to act as a liaison to the Navy shop system that repaired and replaced the parts of Tunny that were broken or worn out.

Usually, most of the repair work was done in the two engine rooms. The snipes were constantly working on Tunny's ancient running gear. Chief Gordon and his men were in the midst of an engine overhaul when Tunny got orders to put to sea. This meant that all the needed spare parts had to be in Tunny's storeroom before she left port. According to Emile Gordon, Tunny was short several main engine bearings, four cylinder liners and several parts to the Fairbanks-Morse vertical drive assembly.

COB had his own shopping list that he was toting around to every Navy shop to "cumshaw" the required spares for the engine rooms. "Cumshaw" is a sailor's term for bartering/stealing. In fact, the definition can be found in the unofficial Bluejackets' Manual. Along with such terms as scuttlebutt, skylarking, and nobber, cumshaw has a very specific meaning to boat sailors. It seems that Chief Vincent was the best at cumshaw. Perhaps this was because he knew where all the "bodies were buried."

Every Navy shop has a Navy supervisor—usually a Chief Petty Officer with that particular shop specialty as his Navy rate. Vincent knew them all because he had served with them at one time or another. COB used this special relationship to expedite Gordon's spare parts procurement and, therefore, Tunny's departure for sea.

Navy Chiefs are the backbone of the service. They have formed their own fraternity forged in the cauldron of conflict. They knew they could rely on each other when the iron is in the fire or when the bureaucracy of the Navy supply system must be bypassed. Because of this personal bond, Tunny was fitted for sea on time and speeding through the waters of the South China Sea on a westerly course that very evening.

David was on watch at the starboard lookout station. He was also taking his final qualifications oral exam from newly promoted LT Oscar Oldham. Oldham was grilling David on the subtleties of Tunny's trim system.

"Okay, Jackson, line up the trim pump to pump from auxiliaries to sea," queried Oldham.

"Open the auxiliary tank suction valve, start the trim pump, and verify that there is pressure on the pump gauge. Then open the main sea valve. Report volume discharge in gallons to the diving officer until ordered to secure pumping." David voice was without any inflection. He parroted the procedure almost as if he were reading from a dictionary. In fact, David could complete the operation he just described in the dark, blindfolded. He had done so in the course of his qualification training.

"Where is the lube oil tank fill valve?" asked Oldham.

"In the After Battery shower. It is operated by a reach-rod valve stem and you have to remove the deck plate aft of the starboard sink to find the valve wheel." David repeated this procedure while peering through binoculars at the horizon.

They had been at the final oral exam for the last six hours. They had started in the wardroom and were forced to continue on the Bridge while on watch. Oscar was OOD and David was starboard lookout. It was dusk and the fading sun was falling below the horizon to Tunny's bow. The sunset was breathtaking. They both stopped to take in the myriad of colors reflected off the clouds and sea.

"Red sky at night, sailors' delight," quoted David.

"Yeah," said Oscar.

They paused in awe at the power of God's creation. Each had seen this sight many times, but it never ceased to bring them a pause. The sheer beauty of sunset at sea could make even the saltiest tar discover religion in their own personal way.

"Well…I guess that does it, Jackson. Hand me your quals card so I can sign you off," Oldham said rather nonchalantly. David reached inside his dungaree shirt and produced his laminated qualifications card. By this time there were a couple of dozen signatures on the card. There was one blank line left to be completed.

Oldham penned his name to the card, handed it back to David, and extended his hand in congratulations. "Well done, sailor! You are now 'qualified in submarines'." David already had a pair of Dolphins he had purchased from a curio vendor in Olongapo. He would pin them to his dungaree shirt at the end of his watch.

The official ceremony was held two days later in the Crews' Mess. David and Simon received their Dolphins in the same ceremony from the Old Man. He presented them with their official Navy issue Dolphins and their qualifications certificate. Tim got his Dolphins three days later.

Roger was two months delinquent in qualifications. He hadn't had a liberty since his run-in at the Rizal street hotel. But he seemed to be taking it in stride. He did his job on Tunny without complaint and he seemed diligent in trying to complete qualifications. Some people are just slower learners than others, he rationalized. He was not especially mechanically adept and his sea-daddy, Snuffy Smith, didn't put a lot of pressure on him to make progress. In fact, Snuffy and Roger shared a special gilly bond.

Roger was the only sailor Snuffy had ever encountered who could keep pace with him while drinking the vile Kaopectate concoction. They shared secret sessions in the Conn while the rest of the crew were in their bunks. They would drink gilly and tell sea stories. Later, Navy doctors would classify them as dependent alcoholics.

That evening, an agent from the Office of Naval Intelligence (ONI) took pictures of Drusilla Gomez meeting with a known Russian KGB agent in a Manila park. The pictures were passed to the CIA liaison at the American Embassy.

Chapter Twenty-Four

Vinh

Tunny surfaced about 600 yards off the coast of North Vietnam—about twenty miles north of the small port city of Vinh. It was slack tide, but the swells approached ten feet. It was the height of the northeast monsoons, causing the unusually large breakers. The day had been overcast and rain had fallen in torrents. Browne had regularly checked the weather through the scope while Tunny lay on the bottom during the daylight hours. He was concerned about tonight's mission when Tunny broke the surface.

It had taken almost six days to make the transit across the South China Sea. The crossing included a stop along side the USS Iwo Jima again. This time the Tunny picked up a platoon of US Marine Recon and their equipment. They also acquired several more IBS's and more of the silent outboard engines, as well.

Only the Old Man and the Marine Platoon Leader knew their mission until they were away from the Iwo. They were to put the Marines ashore near Vinh and wait for their return that next evening. The Marines' mission was kept secret from the crew. However, scuttlebutt being what it is in the Navy, speculation ranged from a training exercise to an attempt to assassinate Ho Chi Minh. None of the scuttlebutt included what was to happen.

Tunny had performed her normal dive after leaving Iwo to trim ship after taking on more crew and material. Upon surfacing the following morning, the Skipper decided to hold a swim call as they were ahead of cruising schedule. During the swim call, a Chinese "fishing boat" spotted them. This particular Chinese craft had no intention of fishing since it didn't have a single net in the water. It was one of their many reconnaissance ships that were in regular contact with all US Navy shipping on duty in Yankee Station.

Tunny and her crew were closely scrutinized and filmed by the Chinese "fishermen." Tunny's crew nonchalantly continued their swim call as if nothing were out of the ordinary. They were in international waters and had every legal right to this location. In fact, Bill Browne, the COB, Oscar Oldham, and several of the crew dropped their trousers and exposed their bare asses to the Chinese film crew in the international display of disdain.

Eventually the fishing boat veered off and apparently went its own way. The radar watch kept the Chinese craft on their scope until they were out of range before Tunny set course for Vinh.

Browne had waited until moonset and slack tide before surfacing to launch the Marines. A submerged launch was impossible. Neither were the Marines trained in lockout procedures nor was it practical for such a large number of men to be locked out through the small escape trunk on Tunny. The time and space constraints made a surface launch the best alternative.

The eight-to-ten foot swells made the launch difficult because the waves kept breaking over Tunny's after deck. As a result, the IBS's were inflated in the hangar before the huge door was opened. However, loading the craft with Marines and their equipment was slowed by the sea conditions. Jackson, Lang, and Roads were detailed to take the Marines to the beach and return with the IBS's. O'Rourke was put in charge of the detail by Browne.

Tunny maneuvered bow on to the beach to present the smallest possible profile to anyone watching from shore. The breakers were washing over Tunny's fantail, thus forcing some of the IBS's back up on deck. The biggest problem was trying to keep the rubber boats stable enough to load men and equipment without losing both overboard.

The plan was to launch twelve boats to land the 40-man Recon platoon. O'Rourke only had four of the outboard engines, so he was forced to lash two boats to a lead boat that was under power. The Tunny Tigers who had been trained in small boat handling would drive the lead boats. They would tow the unpowered craft behind them to the beach and then bring the empty rafts back to Tunny to be stored until signaled by the Marines to be picked up when their mission had been completed.

Finally, O'Rourke got three of the small craft loaded and pushed them away from Tunny's freeboard. Jackson was lead coxswain for these boats and he used his lead boat to assist the others with loading. It took almost 35 minutes to launch the Recon team—a time that was much slower than anticipated. The huge swells and the land-lubbing Marines greatly contributed to the delayed launch.

Once all twelve boats were loaded and away from Tunny, they set a course for the beach. O'Rourke was in the lead boat and he had determined through the periscope before nightfall their course to the beach. There was a tall mahogany tree that stood well above any other beach landmark. O'Rourke had determined that the targeted tree was even visible at night with no moon by watching it through the periscope with Tunny bottomed.

Problems began to compound at this point. There was a strong offshore current that ran perpendicular to their course. The swells continued to increase in height to over twelve feet as they approached the beach. The towed boats began to surf into the powered boats in front of them. The Marines in the powered craft had difficulty keeping their unwanted shipmates from landing in their laps, equipment and all. The under-powered outboards were not strong enough to overcome both the current and the wave action. Furthermore, the four groups of small craft began to separate from each other as a result of the surf conditions.

Jackson lost sight of the boats towed by Roads first. He made a mighty effort to stay in contact with O'Rourke and Tim. They were about 100 yards from the beach and by now completely at the mercy of the surf when they started to draw small arms fire. At first, David thought it was lightening bugs or flying fish.

Then the last boat in his little convoy began to deflate rapidly. The IBS's were compartmentalized so that the loss of one inflatable section did not cause the craft to sink. However, most of the equipment was lost and the boat became a tremendous drag to the progress of the others toward the beach. A couple of Marines in his craft propped their M16's on the bow of his craft and began to return fire.

This action only drew more attention to his boat from the enemy. He could clearly see muzzle flashes now from the tree line above the sandy beach. David shouted to the sinking boat in his towed group. "Pull that last boat to you, bring those guys into your boat and cut that last boat loose! In the bow, stop firing your fucking rifles! You're drawing their fire!"

Once the sinking IBS was cut loose, progress toward the beach was improved. Also, the little engine had an easier job navigating along the shore. David turned with the current and headed up the beach, hopefully away from the incoming fire. By this time he could find neither Tim's boats nor O'Rourke's. He could still hear small arms fire behind his boats and he could see muzzle flashes from the same area.

Jackson grounded the two remaining boats and rushed his crew into the protective cover of the tree line, about 25 yards from the water line. Here he took inventory. He had two wounded Marines, one critically.

He had to get the wounded Marine back to Tunny for evacuation swiftly. However, he was certain that the outboard could not overcome the power of the surf that had caused them so much confusion. Furthermore, he had to locate the remaining Marines and his fellow sailors. He was certain they were in more trouble than his Marines. He talked it over with the Gunnery Sergeant. The Gunny agreed that locating the rest of the platoon was their first priority.

They felt they may have outflanked their antagonists by heading along the coast before landing,. The Gunny felt that by retracing their progress, this time behind the tree line, they could surprise the enemy and find their own men.

Among them they had 10 M16's, twenty grenades, and enough ammunition to make a good showing. They had lost their radio and so had no communication with Tunny. David and a couple of the Marines pulled the remaining two IBS's into the tree line. They searched the two boats for any useful gear and found a box containing flares and a couple of flashlights. There was also a first-aid kit and it was used to comfort the wounded. The critical wound had stopped bleeding.

David and the other wounded Marine agreed to stay behind and guard the IBS's. The Gunny said he would send a detail for them once they linked up with the others in the Recon platoon. They were given two M16's and some ammo "just in case." The Gunny and his men found a trail behind the beach and began heading toward the firing. They soon disappeared into the darkness.

David rearranged the boats and cut some palm fronds to camouflage their position. The three men sought shelter under the camouflaged boats and waited for rescue. In minutes, they heard noises coming from the forest around them. The noises were very subtle and were beginning to strengthen as what ever it was drew closer. The three Americans froze and hardly breathed.

Presently, six khaki-glad figures emerged from the underbrush. They were following the same trail used by Gunny and his men. Their AK47's were unmistakable at the ten-yard distance from the camouflaged rubber rafts and their outnumbered crew. David heard the Marine next to him flip his safety off and move the weapon to full automatic. The NVA heard it too and looked in their direction. A burst of fire exploded from under the raft and two of the enemy went down.

David had hoped to be bypassed by the intruders, but the overzealous jarhead next to him had taken matters in his own hands. Jackson quickly switched his safety off and began firing at the now gone-to-ground enemy. Bullets began to fly wildly over their heads. The Marine had to stop firing to reload.

The remaining VC took advantage of this respite in firing to spring up and charge from their position. It took them only a few seconds to cover the ten yards. Jackson dropped one of them while the Marine reloaded. Suddenly, the NVA were in the boats with them.

They shot the critically wounded Marine before David could respond. He clubbed the nearest NVA with his rifle butt and shoved the barrel of another attacker away before it could be discharged in his face. The full automatic fire from the Marine's reloaded M16 tore his attacker's stomach open. The last of their attackers turned to run back to the forest. David shot one in the back before he reached the shelter of the palms.

They were all covered in blood. The previously critical Marine was dead with a bullet hole in his head. He'd never had a chance. David checked himself for wounds but found nothing more that a burn on his face from the close encounter with the muzzle of an AK47. The surviving Marine had been wounded once more, but this wound could easily be attended to with the remains of the first-aid kit.

Dead NVA lay around them and two more were on the path from which they had first emerged. One of their attackers was still alive; it was the one with his intestines exposed to the sand. He moaned quietly as Jackson turned him over. He was no more than 14 years old. They put the muzzle of an M16 between his eyes and pulled the trigger. His moaning stopped.

The Gunny and the others from David's boat crew reappeared from the palms. The firing had drawn them back. They had not found anyone from their Recon platoon and all firing had stopped up the beach.

They searched the bodies of the fallen enemy and found a few documents. One of which was a map of the beach area around Vinh written in Cyrillic.

Chapter Twenty-Five

Dawn

Mike and Tim looked around now that they could see their surroundings in the gray light of dawn. The firefight had taken its toll on both sides. Two dead Marines lay on the beach among three fully deflated rubber boats. They had landed under heavy fire from the tree line. The Marine Corporal with them could not account for two of his men and the dawn light revealed their fate.

Fortunately, Mike O'Rourke had managed to hang on to a radio and had contacted Tunny with the bad news. The NVA had been laying in ambush for them, it seemed. Somehow their mission had been compromised even before they left for Vinh.

Roger Roads and his twelve Marines hadn't been seen since entering the surf zone. Worse yet, there had been no sign of them all night long. They had heard firing up the beach during the night, but no one could confirm its source or purpose. They presumed it had to do with Jackson's boats, but they had not been able to leave their current position to investigate.

They had managed to assault the tree line once they navigated the surf. They drove off their adversaries and established a position by digging in among a stand of mahogany trees about twenty yards inside the tree line. They had a total force remaining of twenty-one Marines—four of whom were wounded, one critically. The critically wounded was the Marine Lieutenant in charge of the Recon platoon. Mike was now ranking officer.

They were relatively certain that the NVA had suffered casualties, but their comrades had managed to pull the remains of their friends away in the darkness of the previous night. Mike had put in a call to Tunny and been told to hang on till daybreak when they could expect air evacuation.

Mike was really concerned about Roads and Jackson. He had tried to send out patrols, only to have them driven back by enemy opposition. To their credit though, the patrols had located the enemy's positions and were prepared to pinpoint them for an air strike. Navy F4 Phantoms were expected at first light. They were late.

The NVA began a harassing fire that kept the surrounded party of sailors and Marines tucked into their makeshift fortification. Mike began scanning the surrounding forest for signs of the enemy. He was certain that there was someone high in a mahogany tree directing enemy fire. He spotted his nemesis through his binoculars. He called to the Marine corporal, "Marine! You see that sniper in the branches off to out left? He's about thirty feet up in the tree next to the tallest one?"

"Yessir, I see him. Want I should take him out? "

"Yes, with fucking extreme prejudice, Corporal!"

The spotter had revealed his presence by letting light reflect off his binoculars. The Marine lined up on the reflection and fired. Something fell to the ground and the harassing fire from the enemy ceased.

"See any others you want terminated, Lieutenant, just whistle." The corporal winked and returned to help his corpsman with the wounded.

The radio squawked and the Browne's voice came over loud and clear. "Mike, this is Tunny—light your flares now!"

Mike signaled for the flares that would mark their position. They were lit off quickly. They saw the F4's long before they could be heard. They came in from the sea and flew low over their heads. The sound of their powerful engines followed a full three seconds later. The two Phantoms waggled their wings to let the surrounded Americans know they had marked their position.

They banked to starboard and began their bomb run. Khaki-clad NVA emerged from the forest undergrowth and began a hasty evacuation of the area. They had apparently experienced the wrath of Navy F4's before. They were too slow. The napalm canisters fell on top of them as they scurried for cover. Their screams of agony were masked by the sounds of the explosions and the crackle of burning mahogany and human flesh. The smell of gasoline filled the air.

The Marines of Mike and Tim's small force stood and cheered. The F4's made one more run, just for good measure—after all, a carrier landing with unused ordnance was not an acceptable risk.

Tim saw a flare go up down the beach from the approximate location of the previous night's firing. The F4's saw it too and waggled their recognition.

"That's gotta be Jackson, sir!" shouted Tim, "They must have made it, too!"

"Yeah," said Mike, "now all we need to do is locate Roads and his bunch." Mike was not hopeful when it came to those prospects. They had been lost early during the landing. They must have drifted farther down the beach even though they began the approach to the far left of both him and Jackson.

They were nowhere to be found this morning, though. So Mike sent another party up the beach to find Jackson and his beach party. They returned in about 90 minutes with David and the Marines assigned to his boats. All were accounted for—including the dead.

Jackson gave O'Rourke his report quickly and concisely. He, too, was worried about Roger and his crew. Jackson had lost Roads in the surf zone even before they came under fire. Tim thought he had seen Roger's people land, but could not be sure. It had been pretty dark and they were taking fire from a hidden enemy. It had been pure luck that his and Mike's teams had landed so close to each other. Their relative strength in numbers was prominent in securing their small beachhead.

A shout suddenly came from the palm forest. "Hey, Marines, don't shoot! It's us!"

Six beleaguered jarheads emerged and ran into their perimeter. They were dying of thirst and quickly drained a canteen among them. They were from the group for which Roads was responsible. They began to relate their story of the previous night to Mike.

"Well, Lieutenant, we was no more than 100 yards from the beach when we come under fire from the NVA. I'm not too sure about the distance—hard to tell over water like that.

"Anyways, it seemed like a year before we got to the beach. Your sailor tried to turn our bunch around and head back out to sea, but the waves swamped all the boats. They all turned turtle and we lost everything that wasn't fastened to us.

"We swam to the beach individually. I don't think all of us made the beach. I saw one body washing in the surf this morning when the sun came up. We guys hid out under a bunch of driftwood. But your sailor was wavin' his white hanky at the NVA the minute he hit sand last night. The NVA picked him and the rest of our guys up right away. They didn't have no fuckin' chance with that pussy sailor wavin' that tampex like that! Da' Mutherfucker!"

As O'Rourke listened, his Irish temper began flare. "Just how the fuck do you know what was in that sailor's head, swab jockey! He may have been trying to save lives for all you know!"

"Lieutenant, it looked like a cop out to us! After all, we managed to hide out, didn't we?" was the reply.

The Gunnery Sergeant from David's boats agreed to run a recon down the beach with one of the new arrivals to scout for the lost crew. O'Rourke agreed.

Chapter Twenty-Six

Prisoners

Roger had his hands tied behind his back. He had to keep them well up his back to keep from choking himself. A wire noose was wound in the binding on his hands and then around his neck. If he lowered his wrists even a little, he would strangle himself. The wire had already cut a groove in his neck and blood trickled down his chest.

Five of the Marines in his boat party were similarly trussed. One that had been wounded in the previous night's firefight had already strangled himself. He hadn't had the strength to keep slack in the wire around his neck. Once he relaxed his wrists, he slowly choked to death. They had all heard him die—he gurgled and coughed until the wire cut off his windpipe. Even after his death, the wire continued to cut through his throat when his body became completely relaxed. The wire had almost severed his head by dawn. Only the cervical bones held his head to the rest of this body. His head lay at an odd angle on his right shoulder.

The NVA watched with celebration as the Marine died slowly and in agony. They placed bets on the time of his demise. They were consulting the Marine's own watch to confirm the time of his death. Apparently, they already had bets on who would die next.

Roger was terrified. When the boats had swamped and turned turtle, he saw no other choice but to surrender. They had nothing with which to fight, so he found his GI handkerchief and waved it at their antagonists for mercy. The NVA kept on firing for what seemed to be another eternity after he had given up. He just buried his head in the sand of the beach and continued to wave his surrender flag.

Eventually, they had emerged from the tree line and captured

145

their quarry. They treated their prisoners with rude derision. In addition to tying them up so cruelly, they struck them with rifle butts and kicked them as the lay prone. One Marine had been bayoneted. How he managed to live through the night, Roger could not imagine. He was still bleeding from the knife wound in his leg. The loss of blood was beginning to affect his ability to keep slack in his neck wire. He was about to pass out.

One of the other marines yelled at him, "Jimmy! Stay with us! Don't go to sleep! Stay awake, Buddy!"

What Roger and the others saw next was the most terrifying experience of their short lives.

Jimmy opened his eyes and looked around at all his friends. "See you guys in the funny papers, boys!" he said.

His clear blue eyes penetrated each of their hearts as he gave one final jerk with his swollen wrists on the neck wire. The wire quickly severed his throat. He did not die immediately as his body continued to function on the remaining air in his lungs. But he began to convulse from oxygen deprivation.

The NVA howled in celebration. They laughed as Jimmy suffocated in his own blood and money exchanged hands to the winners of the grisly lottery. Jimmy's body finally went slack except for an involuntary twitching of his foot.

Tears filled Roger's eyes. He began to beg for mercy. His cries were met with more laughter and celebration from the NVA. One particularly ugly and scarred Vietnamese specimen walked toward Roger while pulling his knife from his waistband. He reached down and removed Roger's ear with one easy swipe.

At first there was no pain for Roger, it had happened so fast. Only when the NVA began to display his trophy, did Roger realize what had been done. His cries for mercy were replaced by cries of agony. His captors only laughed louder.

They remained trussed in this manner for what seemed hours. Eventually, the pain from Roger's ear began to subside and was replaced by the dull throb of the wire around tightening around his neck. He could feel it slowly slice through the skin of his throat. Any movement only increased the pressure and, therefore, the depth of the wire in his flesh.

He tried to think of other things—his mother, his grandmother, Sarah. He hadn't thought of Sarah in quite awhile. Funny, he thought, now she brings me comfort and she has no idea she is responsible. "I loved you, Sarah. I hope you think of me once in a while."

The ugly NVA rose when he saw Roger's lips moving. He once more removed his knife as he advanced upon Roger. Just then, the NVA's chest exploded. It was followed almost immediately by the sounds of more M16's. The NVA who were gathered around their little cooking fire tried to grab their weapons, but it was too late. The Gunny and his crew were upon them in seconds. They died with the same mercy shown their prisoners. Not one of them escaped with his life.

The Recon Marines quickly untied their comrades and tended their wounds. Roger's ear received a bandage and the wire cut was disinfected with antiseptic. They gathered what they could salvage and began to return to O'Rourke's beachhead fortification. Among the dead NVA, they found a Russian officer dressed in an NVA uniform. His identification said he was a colonel in the KGB. They retrieved his body and took it with them back to Tunny. His grisly carcass would be zipped into a body bag and placed in Tunny's frozen meat locker for the return voyage.

Chapter Twenty-Seven

Rescue

The arrival of the missing Marines caused a brief celebration among the beached Americans. They had been waiting for the return of the recon patrol to call for extraction. Captain Browne had a mike boat standing by for them. An LST was in the area on other transport business and assigned the mike boat to Tunny for the day to recover the stranded Marine platoon.

A mike boat (LCM) was nothing more than a reinforced Higgins Boat made famous during the World War II landings in the Pacific and on D-Day. The landing craft could easily handle the rescue mission, but would not have been suitable for a clandestine nighttime landing. The six-cylinder Detroit diesel engine that was its main propulsion was too noisy. Also, its high profile made it easy to spot from the beach.

However, since this mission had obviously gone awry, Browne wanted his crew and the Marines assigned to him out of harms' way quickly. The mike boat was perfect for the rescue of his crew.

As the mike boat approached the beach, the coxswain revved the diesel, forcing the craft as far up the beach as possible to facilitate the recovery. The ramp was released and fell in almost dry sand. The wounded were the first to be loaded. David and Tim were detailed to deflate the IBS's and set them ablaze along with anything else that would assist the enemy.

David used a K-bar knife to puncture the remaining boats. Air was quickly released and the rubber crafts were stacked upon each other as diesel fuel doused the pile. Tim used a flare to ignite the bonfire as David piled on more of the useless rubber boats.

They policed the area for anything else the NVA could use, including the expended brass from their M16's. Things that wouldn't burn were thrown into a canvas ditty bag to be taken back to Tunny for disposal at sea. The dead were loaded last; including the dead Russian agent.

David and Tim lingered to ascertain that all was ablaze before they headed for the mike boat. Tim turned on the ramp to take one last look at the fire before boarding. David caught the reflection of the scope from a sniper's rifle out of the corner of his eye. He saw the puff of powder smoke before he heard the report of the rifle. His cry of warning came too late. The sniper's bullet entered Tim's chest on his right side and exited from his lower back. Tim fell to the deck of the mike boat almost as if his feet had been knocked from under him.

David rushed to his aid and pulled him into the safety of the boat. A Marine Corporal opened up with his rifle, but no one would ever be certain that he killed Tim's killer. Tim looked up at David and pulled his ear down to his mouth.

"Tell Alice that I'm sorry—it was all my fault. Tell her I love her." Some had heard the death rattle before—that sound a dying person makes as they expire. They seem to be clinging to life for one last breath. Tim struggled against death for only moments, then he surrendered to it. He exhaled a goodbye in David's ear.

David never told anyone in Tunny's crew what Tim's last words were. Tears filled his eyes as Mike pulled him away from Tim's lifeless form.

Chapter Twenty-Eight

Betrayal

An ONI agent met Tunny as she tied up at Rivera Pier. He had been alerted via radio to meet the boat when she docked. Tunny's Skipper informed the ONI that he had something they might find valuable.

Bill gave the Cyrillic-encrypted map and Russian identification documents to the intelligence agent. The KBG agent's body was mysteriously spirited away by a couple of people in civilian clothes. Only a few would ever know what exactly became of the remains. To Bill's surprise, the ONI agent asked to see Simon Berg. They both left Tunny in a black staff car.

Simon was taken to an obscure Quonset hut at Cubi Point Naval Air Station. He was escorted into a lime-green painted room that contained nothing but a long table and a few folding chairs painted government-issue gray. He was asked to take a seat while the ONI agent opened a manila file on the table.

"My name is Thomas Stevens. I'm a Navy Commander with the Office of Naval Intelligence. For the record, please state your name, rank, and serial number."

"I am Third-class Petty Officer Simon Berg, serial number B300215. What's all this about?"

"Do you know a Miss Drusilla Gomez, Petty Officer Berg?"

"Yes sir, I do. What does that have to do with this?"

"Did you place a call to Miss Gomez the day before you left for your last deployment?" asked Stevens.

"I believe I did. What business is that of yours, sir?"

"What is your relationship with Miss Gomez, Berg?" Stevens was beginning to become belligerent.

"As I said," barked Simon, "it's none of your God-damn business what my relationship is with Drusilla. Your insinuations are disgusting, Commander Stevens."

"Do you know or are you familiar with one Andre' Popov? Have you ever met or corresponded with the aforementioned Mr. Popov?" Stevens voice and manner was now condescending.

"What the fuck are you implying, sir? The only Popov I know comes from a bottle and is a cheap substitute for the real thing. What does your friend Popov have to do with Drusilla and me, anyway?" Simon returned the condescension quickly.

Suddenly, Drusilla was there. She walked through the door as if she were comfortably living in her own home.

"Is this the man you talked with, Miss Gomez?" asked Stevens.

"Yes, this young fool is the source of so much of my information. His letters and phone calls have been of great assistance to us." It was as if she were a stranger to Simon, not his one true love.

"What are you talking about, Dru? What information? Have I missed something here? Have I been used?" Simon was astonished and shocked. Things began to fall into place for him. Was Drusilla a spy?

"Well, Goddamn it!" he shouted. "Have I been used? Have you taken something from me and used it to do damage to my friends and shipmates?"

"You love-sick fool! Of course I have. That's my job and you made it so easy for me, you horny little Jew! All I did was show you a little cleavage and a shapely ass and I had you slobbering all over yourself. You Americans are so predictable. The promise of a little pussy and you would have told me the secrets of nuclear physics, had I wanted." Now Drusilla was condescending.

Simon fell back in his chair. He turned white as blood drained from his face and felt dizzy. He slowly got up to leave the room. As he got to the door, he stopped and turned on his heel. He faced Drusilla and bent down to put his face in front of hers.

"No, you're wrong Drusilla. I stole something from you, if you ever had anything to steal. I took your integrity. I took your honor. We Americans may appear foolish and love-struck to you, but we are willing to give to each other that which you will never possess.

"I gave you the greatest gift one person can give another—love, unquestioning love. Now you have nothing—you lost my love and

I took your honor from you just now. Oh, I'll find another person to love and trust blindly one day. But you never will—you're too cynical for that! How can you ever trust someone now? How can they ever trust you?

"No, Drusilla, you are the loser here today. I have a future, you have only the thoughts of lost love. I hope you can cuddle up with that thought on a cold winter's night in your prison cell."

Simon pulled the door open and walked through. Only then did his eyes fill with tears.

Stevens later explained everything to Browne, Berg, and the rest of Tunny's officers. Apparently, the enemy had been keeping tabs on Tunny's movements for several months. Berg's infatuation with Drusilla Gomez was pure serendipity for the Russians and their Vietnamese allies. The KGB agent killed in the Vinh operation was the very one photographed with Drusilla Gomez in Manila. He had been identified from the photographs taken by the ONI. They had been keeping Drusilla Gomez under surveillance for the last several months.

Vinh was a base of supply for the Viet Cong. Vinh's access to the Gulf of Tonkin made it ideal as a jumping off point for contraband shipped on small Vietnamese watercraft—junks. In addition, there had been a POW camp close ashore. The Marine Recon's mission was to locate the contraband for destruction by naval air forces and free the POW's. After the failed landing, it was revealed that the POW's were removed to Hanoi and placed in the infamous Hanoi Hilton prisoner-of-war camp.

The NVA were well aware of the strategic importance of the Vinh warehouses and had used the POW's as a screen against possible air strikes by US Naval aircraft. The combination of Simon's information through Drusilla and Popov, Russian satellite photos of Tunny alongside Iwo Jima, and the photos taken by the Chinese "fishermen" all served to tip the enemy off as to Tunny's intended mission. The NVA had been waiting in ambush for the landing party for at least two nights before Tunny's crew had attempted their landing.

Simon was given a reprimand by the Commander of Submarine Flotilla Seven and lost his secret clearance for a period of six months. The worst part was his knowledge that his complacence and blind trust may have cost his friend his life, as well as the lives of the Marines assigned to Tunny's latest patrol. He would have to live with that guilt for the rest of his life.

Chapter Twenty-Nine

Coming Home

Tim's body and those of the dead Marines had been interred to the deep on the passage back to Subic Bay. The crew had gathered on Tunny's after deck as Bill Browne eulogized the fallen sailor and Marines.

"We commend the bodies if these souls departed to the sea in the sure and certain knowledge…"

David and the other Tunny shipmates manned the submarine's leeward side in their dress white uniforms and stood at attention as Captain Browne read the eulogy. The words of the Navy Hymn came to David as he watched Tim's body slide off the pall and into the calm sea.

"God hear us when we send to thee
For those in peril on the sea…"

Then the waters of the South China Sea closed her arms around Tim and those that had given their lives in service to their country.

The return trip was solemn and even morose. Roger and those wounded with him were transported to a hospital ship in Saigon harbor; and then later to Oakland Naval Hospital. Browne had been right—Roger would never return to submarine duty, let alone complete his service obligation. His mother met him in Oakland, had him medically discharged, and took him home to Hollywood. None of Tunny's crew ever saw him again, even at ship reunions.

David made a trip to Manila two days after Tunny docked. He was met by Alice at the bus station. She took his hand as they walked toward the Peace Corps van.

"His last words were of you, Alice. He pulled me down and told me to tell you it was his fault and that he loved you."

"You know David, in a way, he really died that night with Katy. He never recovered from that awful night. Somehow, Ansel killed him, too. Not mercifully like he did Katy—he took his soul from him and Burris died a little every day after that."

"No, Alice. That's not right. If Burris died with Katy, then Tim was reborn in Tunny. You didn't know him like Simon, Roger, and I knew him. You couldn't be expected to…you didn't share a fellowship of arms that we had…still have."

David reached in his pocket and retrieved the shining insignia of submarine sailors.

"One last thing—only he and your father knew who actually shot Ansel. It was Burris. He let Fred Lang take the rap and Burris felt guilty for the rest of his life. He felt he killed your brother out of rage and revenge. Burris never forgave himself for that. But Tim was free of the killing. It was Burris that shot Ansel. Tim had a clean soul and a clear conscience, if you will."

Alice interrupted, "Then I must have reminded him of what he thought was his wrongdoing! He didn't ever do anything wrong in my eyes, even if it was him that shot Ans. Why didn't he tell me the truth, David? I would have understood! Didn't he know that?"

"Alice, you don't get it. Tim, your Burris, was a gentlemen and it was in his upbringing to protect those in his care. You and Katy were his responsibility. He always felt he betrayed you both that night Ansel died. Burris could never forgive himself. But, in a strange way, Tim was never there.

"He asked that I give these to you. Tim earned them on our last trip, just before he was killed."

David slid Tim's Dolphins into Alice's hand. She looked down at the silver embossed insignia of submariners and tears flowed from her eyes. She laid her head on David's shoulder for a moment to gather her emotions. He took her hand and they walked to the car.

Epilogue

Emily Browne sat in the car patiently waiting on Bill, as she had done countless times before. They were parked at Rivera Pier, Berth One. Bill had forgotten a few things in the wardroom that he would need on his next duty assignment.

Bill, Emily, and Bill Jr. had been transferred to one of the new nuclear submarines under construction at Mare Island Naval Shipyard in Vallejo, California. They were leaving the next day from Clark Air Force Base.

A white-clad form appeared from behind her and staggered to Tunny's gangway. She recognized the sailor. It was that drunken Quartermaster, Smith. He was obviously drunk again. "Oh, well," she thought, "I guess his demotion to Third Class Petty Officer had no impact on his problem."

She watched as Smith negotiated the prow and walked across the fore deck without stopping, straight into Subic Bay. It was like one of those scenes from a comic opera. The Topside Watch threw the life buoy at Smith as he surfaced close aboard. Emily burst into spontaneous laughter.

"Smith never could navigate in port, I guess," she said to young Bill. He was asleep in the back seat, so she spoke mostly to herself.

Just then Bill and Gary Barker appeared from the Forward Room companion way. Bill was in civvies and Gary was dressed in his khakis. A brand new Command-at-Sea badge was pinned above Gary's left breast pocket. The ceremony transferring command had taken place that afternoon. Bill had recommended Gary for the job when they were offered the new boat. It had been only Emily's urging that had convinced Bill to relinquish command of Tunny. Bill would have served another tour as Captain of that old scow, she believed.

They had fought over the offered transfer. It was one of the most unpleasant fights of their married life. She glanced out the passenger window at Tunny. She was again moored port-side to the pier. Somehow, this bilious configuration of iron and steel had captured Bill's heart. No—she reconsidered that thought. It was the crew of Tunny that had captured his heart. Tunny was only the cathedral that brought them together.

Most of the original crew were gone now. Some had served their time, like Mike O'Rourke. He was in San Diego now; in partnership with his brother-in-law running a saloon on Broadway. He had re-married, she understood, to his former wife. Emily didn't give that union much chance to survive, but everyone deserves a second chance, she thought.

Mike had received a Bronze Star with a V for valor for that nasty mission that had killed young Tim Lang. Lang had received his Navy Achievement Medal and Purple Heart Medal posthumously. Bill had awarded them to his sister at a ceremony on Tunny's foredeck a month after they had returned to Subic. The other member of Tunny's crew that received a medal that day had been transferred to another submarine in Key West. She had heard from scuttlebutt that Lang's sister had followed him there. She wished she could remember that young man's name—he had been so handsome in his dress whites at the award ceremony. She would ask Bill when he got back to the car.

Bill shook Gary Barker's hand as he walked to the gangway. Even in civvies and out of force of habit, Bill saluted the flag as he left Tunny for the last time.

She heard the announcement over the 1MC, "Tunny—Departing!"

Bill turned and looked back down at Barker. She would swear years later that she detected a tear in his eye. He was no longer Captain of Tunny, so the announcement was in tribute and no longer required protocol.

The base cab almost ran Bill down as it pulled to a stop at Tunny's gangway. Two white-clad sailors with seaman apprentice stripes on their left sleeves disembarked from the rear seat. They hoisted their seabags and walked to the edge of the pier.

"This the Tunny?" one inquired of the Topside Watch.

"Fresh meat," thought Emily in amusement. The Old Girl was

getting new crew. She would be their home now. She would be a hard task-master and they would be forced to learn all about her. But she would test their character and courage—and if they passed her tests, they would come to love her as Bill did now.

Bill pulled the car door open and piled into the driver's seat.

"I told Gary that he could pick the car up at our old quarters tomorrow. I'll leave the keys on the kitchen counter in the vain hope that one of those giant Philippine cockroaches won't devour them."

He looked over at Emily and saw the tears in her eyes. She was watching the new crewmen board Tunny with their new seabags, shiny new shoes, and youthful innocence. Bill knew how she felt.

"Don't worry, Baby. They'll be fine. Gary and Oscar are there to see that they survive. The COB will deride 'em just like he did all those that came before. They'll be better men for the experience, don't you know."

"That's not why I'm crying, Bill. Look at her." Emily gestured out her window. "She is the ugliest ship in the harbor and at the same time the most beautiful. She's like an ugly child that only a mother could love.

"But it's like I'm seeing her for the first time. So much has happened to her and so many have served her. How can we leave her here in this awful place? She is like a mother to us, now."

Bill Browne was astonished. "Emily, that's the way all sailors feel about the ships we serve in. I didn't think you understood. They protect us from the deep and they shelter us from the storms and they work their way into our hearts. It doesn't matter if the ship is a PT Boat or the Enterprise, sailors fall in love with them. Not a day will pass from now on that each of Tunny's crew will not think of her—no matter when they served her. She's part of them now—and always will be."

Bill started the car and put it in gear. He depressed the accelerator and turned away from the pier. Emily turned back in her seat to listen to the new crewmen report in. The sound of their young voices grew faint as Tunny disappeared in the fog.

THE END